THE GOLD BONANZA

Loping along the trail, old prospector Dusty Morgan literally falls headlong into a bonanza — a lost Aztec goldmine. Desperate to share the news of his good fortune, despite knowing he should keep quiet, he confides in saloon girl Val Kent. But can she be trusted? And there are other eyes watching and other ears listening: saloon owner Drew Carson and his unscrupulous gunhawk. Meanwhile, a ruthless Aztec woman, Maninza, regards the gold as her rightful ancestral property . . .

JOHN RUSSELL FEARN

THE GOLD BONANZA

Complete and Unabridged

LINFORD
Leicester

First published in Great Britain in 1950
as *Aztec Gold* by John Russell Fearn

First Linford Edition
published 2016

All the characters and events in this book are
fictitious; any resemblance to a real person or
circumstance is unintentional.

A catalogue record for this book is available
from the British Library.

ISBN 978–1–4448–2895–5

Published by
F. A. Thorpe (Publishing)
Anstey, Leicestershire

Set by Words & Graphics Ltd.
Anstey, Leicestershire
Printed and bound in Great Britain by
T. J. International Ltd., Padstow, Cornwall

This book is printed on acid-free paper

1

'Git movin', yuh ornery cuss afore I kicks th' daylights outa yuh!'

Being accustomed to this kind of threat, Dusty Morgan's mule took no notice. He sat solidly on his haunches, his front legs spread wide and something close to a laugh on his long face.

'Gosh durn it, what's gotten inter yuh?' the old prospector demanded, pushing up his filthy old Stetson on to his moist forehead. 'There ain't no more'n fifteen miles t'go t' Hell's Acres an' some comfort, an' yuh sit here solid.'

The mule remained obdurate. Dusty Morgan pushed his hat higher and scratched his grey head. He was sixtyish, hard as rock, a prospector and a wanderer who had never given up hope of happening upon a bonanza one day. He had friends in every town in

1

Arizona. He lived his life in the open and travelled far — when the mule was congenial. At moments like this the animal made him see red. Dry as a kiln from thirst, Dusty's only ambition at the moment was to reach Hell's Acres — a dim smudge in the shimmering violet of the horizon at the moment — and drink beer until he could drink no more.

'Mebbe I should ha' gotten me a hoss,' the old man mused, squinting into the cloudless cobalt-blue of the sky. 'None uv this obstinacy then — ' He moved to the animal and pulled off the bedroll and neatly folded prospector's equipment, but although lightened somewhat of his load the mule remained seated.

'Listen, feller . . . ' The prospector went down on his knees and looked into the mule's vague eyes. 'This sun ain't gittin' no higher an' the night's a-comin'. You an' me both need ter bed down, see? Fur th' luv of old Dusty Morgan will yuh please git on yuh blasted *feet*?'

Perhaps it was the yell in the last word which did it. Anyway nobody was more surprised than Dusty when the animal suddenly stood up and began moving. The old man began moving too — mighty fast — to get the bedroll and pans and paraphernalia back in place as the animal refused to stand still. Finally, gasping and cursing, Dusty struggled into the saddle and muttered sourly to himself as the mule moved along at a jog-trot, stirring a cloud of dust into the blistering sunlight.

It was around late afternoon in the spring of the year, the time when the deserts and mesa were alive with colour and the pastures were smothered under the loco-weeds and brittle-bush. The breeze was hot and dry, filled with a multitude of aromas. Dusty Morgan had smelled them for so many years they no longer registered. It took a townsman, who had never been in this wild beauty before, to appreciate the glory of it.

Or perhaps it was that the old

prospector was not in the mood to appreciate *anything*. For many long weeks, ever since the winter rains had stopped, he had been prowling around Arizona on his ceaseless quest for a bonanza. Not that he worked at random, either. He knew, in common with other prospectors, that abandoned gold mines were to be found all over Arizona, relics of the dynasty of the Aztecs, but so well hidden that few save the Redskins themselves knew exactly where to look. Dusty knew quite well that he might search in vain all his life; but on the other hand —

'Well, take what's a-comin' ter me, I guess,' he sighed, as the mule continued loping along. 'Mebbe I'll wind up rich; mebbe I'll finish up beside a bonanza an' not know th' thing's there.'

He fell to reflection again. He had a little gold dust he could use for drink and a few nights rest under cover — gold which he had obtained the hard way, panning at one of the mountain streams. Little enough return for months of work. There'd be just time for him to see a few of the familiar faces in Hell's Acres, then off again to —

'Hey, what th' hell — !' he burst out, and found himself suddenly flying over the mule's head.

Unexpectedly the animal had caught its forefeet against an upstanding chunk of rock in the badly defined trail. Dusty Morgan had no chance to save himself. He landed with dizzying impact in the dust — and then fell again, tumbling helplessly into darkness amidst a rain of rock chippings and choking clouds of grit and sand.

Shaken, his eyes smarting, he came to a halt on his back. It took him a few moments to realize no bones were broken. Cursing painfully he got on to his knees and then stood up. To his surprise there was darkness all around him and a hole about nine feet overhead. Framed in the hole was the head of the mule, his teeth bared in that semblance of an idiotic grin.

'All right, durn yuh hide, laugh!' the

old man snorted. 'It ain't so dad-blamed funny as you seem t'think — Anyways,' he broke off, looking about him, 'where in heck am I?'

Curiosity had him now. It only took him a few seconds to grasp that the fall had caused him to smash through a very thin crust of rock in the trail and down into this — What? He began searching hurriedly for matches, struck one, and peered around in the yellow, wavering glimmer.

Just as he saw something which made his throat go even drier than before, the match flame scorched his fingers and expired. He went forward a few paces, struck another match, and gazed again.

Gold! Not just a vein of it in the rocks — though that would have been magnificent enough — but chunks of it embedded deep in its natural bed of quartz. It lay in all directions, heaped in cairns in this long deserted cavern. Little nuggets of it were scattered about the floor.

'Sweet sufferin' bells, I'm goin'

crazy,' Dusty muttered; then just as quickly knew that he was not. Just the same he stood for some moments in the dark, assimilating the incredible fact that his life's dream had abruptly come true. He had struck a bonanza. Gold — *gold* — enough of it to destroy all his cares for the rest of his life.

More matches — more peering — then he picked up a small nugget and examined it. His experienced eye told him immediately there was no fake about it. Genuine yellow metal. Startled, feeling he wanted to round run in circles or yell at the top of his voice, he pushed the nugget in his hip pocket and then considered how best to get out of this treasure trove.

He managed it with a long jump which racked his old bones pretty badly. Wealth and excitement had given him superhuman strength, though, and with a dirty, sweat-covered face he finally scrambled over the ledge of the hole he had made and began a war-dance round the impartial mule.

7

'Look at it, feller!' he yelled, showing the nugget to the disinterested animal. 'A bellyful fur you and a fortune fur me. We made it, pardner! We made it!' And he flung his arm round the creature's neck and kissed the rigid face affectionately.

Then Dusty's immediate excitement began to abate. He became once more the wily old man who had lived for years in these wastes and knew every trick. Very deliberately he set to work to cover up the traces of his activities. It took him two hours, but at the end of that time the gap in the ancient trail was covered with brambles and branches from the nearby vegetation, and over that again, lay a carpet of rock chippings interwoven with leaves, sand, and dust. Anybody coming right over the spot would inevitably fall through the cover, of course — but the chance of it happening was remote. He had fallen off the actual trail and only those who wandered the range, as Dusty always did, would be likely to discover the bonanza, and that would be a slight risk. In any case it was a chance the old man was prepared to take, it was unlikely anyone would fall off a second time!

'Yeah, an' what happens now?' he muttered, scratching his wiry chin and squinting at the much lowered sun. 'Ain't no fun in keepin' a thing like this to yuhself — yet I'd be plumb loco ter spit it out where a lot uv jiggers could horn in on me . . . '

For a moment he was baffled. It was only human for him to wish to advertise his good news after so many years of failure yet with the number of chisellers and gunhawks there were around he might sign his own death warrant if he talked. Then he grinned and patted the mule's nose gently.

'Guess we forgot Val Kent, feller,' he said. 'She's a nice kid, an' I'd stake my boots she wouldn't tell anybody if I asked her not to.'

In this Dusty probably underestimated Valerie Kent, but she was certainly a safer bet than most of the people he could think of in Hell's Acres — whither he was heading. The fact remained he *had* to tell *somebody* before he exploded, and Valerie Kent had always been a friend of his — much in the fashion as a daughter might have been, had he ever got around to marrying.

'Let's go!' Dusty decided abruptly, and clambered back into the saddle.

To his relief the mule did not try any tricks with the resullt that the weary miles still to be covered before Hell's Acres was reached were progressively diminished. Nevertheless it was night-fall by the time the rickety old township was reached.

It lay at the base of the Paradise Mountains, a ramshackle conglomeration of wooden buildings, predominant amongst which were a saloon — The Last Frontier — a general store, a livery stable, and a tabernacle. Through the midst of the huddled buildings, all of them designed without any regard for the finer details of architecture, ran the main street. In the dry weather it was a vista of foot-thick dust: in the rainy season a quagmire . . . It was a town which had grown up bit by bit as ranchers and settlers had drifted into the region. In its way it was prosperous, especially for those who were quick on the draw.

It was no new vision to Dusty as he surveyed it upon his approach. It looked the same to him as it had ever done, the kerosene street lights flaring, the horses fastened to the tie-racks outside the saloon, the men and women moving along the the boardwalks.

'Yeah, town don't look a bit different,' Dusty commented to his mule, and spat trail dust from his mouth. 'None uv these hick towns ever does . . . '

He nodded to one or two punchers whom he recognized as they signalled a greeting from the boardwalk; then he slipped from the saddle, tethered the mule to the tie-rack, and wandered into the clogged and smoky atmosphere of

11

The Last Frontier.

To commence with he had no eyes for anybody. The batwings were still swinging from his entry by the time he had reached the bar-counter and ordered beer. He drank it straight back, paid for it in gold dust, and then stood looking about him as he wiped the back of his hand over his mouth.

'Looks like you were dry, old-timer,' a voice remarked.

Dusty glanced up at the big figure of Drew Carson, owner of The Last Frontier. Though he had a smile there was hardness in his blue eyes. Though his manner was genial there was a tautness in it as though he lived perpetually on guard. In point of fact he did. His gun gave him virtual control over Hell's Acres — though he took good care never to cross the sheriff or mayor — and his finances he expanded by occasional ventures into masked banditry, robbing trains or stage coaches when it was worth his while. So far he had got away with it . . . So far.

'Sure was dry,' the prospector agreed, and shook the saloon owner's big hand as he held it out. 'Kind uv excited too, I guess. That makes yuh drier.'

'Yeah.' The expression on Drew Carson's bronzed, lean face did not change. 'Excited, feller? What about?'

Dusty grinned, exposing toothless gums, and instead of answering ordered another drink. Since Carson knew better than try and probe the hardbitten old devil he did not repeat the question — but nevertheless his interest was stirred. Dusty obviously *was* excited — more so than he had ever been, and when a man lives or dies by finding gold it seemed more or less logical to Carson that yellow metal might be the answer.

'Have another drink?' he invited, as Dusty drained his glass for the second time.

'Nope — I reckon not. Yuh might give me so much I'd get tight an' then I'd start talkin'. That I ain't aimin' t'do. No, sir!'

13

'Talking?' The saloon owner grinned disarmingly. 'What have you got to talk about?'

'Like t'know, wouldn't yuh?' The old prospector thrust out his whiskery chin obstinately. 'Nothin' doin', feller — '

Still Drew Carson had no expression beyond his bland smile. That he was irritated was evident to nobody save himself. He could sense something big was brewing somewhere and this old fool had the answer.

'Don't see the gal no place,' Dusty muttered, half to himself, after a long survey of the smoky room.

'What gal?' Carson asked, surprised, lighting a cheroot.

'Val Kent. Been some months since I was last here. She ain't blown town, has she?'

'When she does I'll lose plenty of customers,' Carson assured him. 'No, she's still around — just dressin' after her number. She'd just finished singing when you blew in.' And as the old man made no comment Carson asked,

14

'What d'you want with her, anyways? Can't be yore in love with her — at your age.'

'S'posin' I wus?' Dusty asked, with his leathery grin.

'I mightn't like it, old timer. She means a lot to me does Val and I don't like anybody hornin' in. Anyways,' the saloon owner added, smiling, 'I guess any opposition you can put up won't count for much.'

Dusty pondered this in silence for a moment, then he gave a little start as he caught sight of Valerie Kent emerging between the dark curtains at the far end of the saloon. Without so much as a glance back at the saloon owner the old prospector headed towards her, shambling his way between the tables and nodding acknowledgement wherever he glimpsed a familiar face.

Valerie Kent saw him coming — and smiled. She was a tallish, good-looking girl in her late twenties, makeup helping to diminish the faults which prevented her being a beauty. Her mouth was

15

perhaps a little too large; her nose a trifle too long — but otherwise there were few men who did not find her attractive. Even her habitual coolness of manner — an attitude she had adopted as a safeguard in this land of tough wanderers — did not prevent her being altogether likeable.

'Val.' The old prospector reached her and grasped her slim hand as she held it out in greeting. 'I thought fur th' minnit yuh'd walked out and it came as a mighty shock! Then Carson back there told me you wus still around — How's tricks, gal? Dang me if yuh ain't still as purty as ever!'

'Thanks, Dusty.' Val gave him one of her kindest smiles. She had always had a liking for the hard-bitten old dirt-washer who seemed to regard her as he might his own daughter. 'Just the same I'm getting a bit tired of being stuck around here. It can get monotonous being Drew Carson's singer, you know.'

Dusty looked about him upon the

faro and roulette tables, the men playing poker, the over-painted women drinking — Then he came close to spitting in contempt but seemed to think better of it.

'No place fur a gal like you,' he decided. 'But anyways that ain't none uv my business. If yuh ever walk out I'll be mighty sorry — Be sure ter leave word where yuh go, won't yuh, specially if yuh marry some up-an'-comin' rancher.'

The girl laughed. 'Not much chance of that, Dusty. I guess Drew has had me fixed ever since I strayed in here from back east. Not that I mind,' she reflected. 'He's not so bad.'

'Not so bad nothing,' the old man objected, with a glance back through the tobacco fumes to where the saloon owner was still standing beside the bar and talking with some of his immediate colleagues.

'Well — now what?' Valerie asked, question in her grey eyes. 'Anythin' more beyond shaking hands? I suppose you'll be on your way again almost immediately?'

'Mebbe — mebbe not. I've somethin' to show yuh, Val. An' I wouldn't show it anybody else. Come right over here an' let me buy you a drink.'

Val shrugged and raised no objections as Dusty found an empty corner table and settled her in it. He ordered drinks from the laconic waiter and then waited until they bad been brought. This done he looked at the girl intently.

'Afore I go any further,' he said, 'I want yuhr promise that you won't say anythin' to anybody about what I'm goin' ter tell yuh.'

'All right,' Val agreed, quite casually.

Seeing no reason to doubt the girl who was his only woman friend Dusty fished the nugget from his pocket and laid it on the table, using his horny hand as a shield about it so nobody at the neighbouring tables could see his prize.

'Nice, ain't it?' he grinned. 'Same colour as your hair, gal, I reckon.'

'Gold,' Valerie whispered, fingering the nugget but taking care not to raise it. 'Where on earth did you find it?'

'That I ain't sayin', Val.' The old man's whiskery chin had set obstinately. 'Not becos I don't trust you, but yuh might accidentally let it slip if I gave yuh the details — an' I don't intend to take that chance. Later, when I've made my plans, I might be able t'help yuh git away from this pesthole. I guess all yuh need to do it is money, and th' way I'm figgerin' things I should have plenty before long.'

'Even if you did tell me, Dusty, you don't suppose I'd be idiot enough to let it slip, do you?' the girl demanded, her eyes bright at the thought of a fortune within her grasp if only she could make the old man loosen up. 'It wouldn't be worth my while to let anything slip — Come on, let me into it. You've found a bonanza somewheres, haven't you?'

'I sure have — an' I wouldn't be tellin' yuh about it at all only I just had to — or blow up. I reckon that after yuh've bin searchin' fur years fur a gold mine, and not discoverin' it, yuh just can't keep it to yuhself when yuh succeed. But I don't aim to be crazy enough to tell where it is. No, sir! Not even t'you, Val.'

He saw her face harden a little but affected not to notice. Over at the counter Drew Carson stood frowning, his heavy figure propped against the bar as his drawn-back elbows rested on it.

'I don't get it,' he muttered, and the man on his right — one of his own particular gunhawks — gave him a questioning glance.

'What's wrong, boss?'

'Dusty Morgan over there,' Carson growled, nodding towards him. 'The crafty old jigger's got something on his mind. I never saw him so het up before — but he's cagey enough not to give himself away. Whatever secret it is he's got he seems t'be handin' it on to Val.'

'Which makes it easy,' his gunhawk grinned. 'Let him go on tellin' her, then later on yuh can beat th' infurmation outa her in your own good time.'

Carson gave him a sour look. 'Any more cracks like that from you, Pete, an' I'll kick your teeth out. I never beat a gal in my life an' I don't aim t'do it now.'

'Y'might, if it wus worth your while. I guess Val Kent ain't the kind uv gal to say anythin' she don't wanter of her own free will — '

'The old jigger's got something on that table,' Carson interrupted, watching keenly. 'Hidden by his hand.'

'Yeah.' Pete looked too, his eyes narrow. 'Sure looks like it — what I can see fur this blasted tobacco smoke.'

Both of them moved their eyes abruptly to a girl who had just entered the saloon. She moved gracefully — a lithe, black-haired girl in her mid-twenties, her copper skin enhanced by the scarlet riding shirt she was wearing. Controlled strength was packed into her rounded limbs, which her close-fitting black riding pants revealed to perfection. Maninza was no stranger to The Last Frontier even though few spoke to her. A descendant of the Aztecs she was a law unto herself — inscrutable, cultured, and the owner of the huge Lazy-J ranch a couple of miles from Hell's Acres. Every evening she made her visit, indulged a soft drink, and then went out again without hardly a word.

As on all other occasions she moved now straight to the bar, ordered her drink, and stood looking about her, the light catching the sheen of her black hair, her slightly oblique dark eyes studying the saloon's habituees and then coming back to contemplate Drew Carson.

'Evenin', ma'am,' he greeted, and touched his big Stetson.

She nodded calmly, her face expressionless, the high cheekbones accentuating its immobility.

'I guess that dame gives me the creeps,' Pete confided, his voice low. 'I reckon she'd put a knife in yuh ribs as soon as look at yuh.'

'Stop botherin' about her an' go an' find out what Dusty's doing,' Carson told him. 'I don't care how you do it but break it up. I don't fancy that dirty old *hombre* hangin' around Val as he does.'

Pete nodded and, hands in his trousers pockets, lounged casually across the saloon. He walked far more unsteadily than normal — deliberately, conveying the impression he could not hold his liquor. Carson watched him go, grinning a little to himself — and so did Maninza, but on her face there was no smile. Her eyes merely watched, dispassionately, her darkly tanned fingers playing with her glass on the counter.

'Howdy, pardner!' Pete greeted loudly, as he came up behind the prospector. 'Ain't seen yuh in some time — !'

He delivered a resounding slap on the back, the violence of which was sufficient to make the old man lurch forward helplessly. The table rocked. The glasses upset and poured their contents into

Val's lap as she leapt up in fury. The gold nugget dropped to the floor and rolled a few feet. In one frenzied dive Dusty was after it, but Pete got there first and picked it up. 'Gimme that,' the old prospector yelled. 'Blast yuh eyes, *gimme*!' And he literally tore it from Pete's palm.

Pete did not step out of character. He grinned stupidly and circled an arm over his head.

'Sorry, old timer — an' you, Miss Val. I guess I didn't — '

'Get away from here!' Val nearly screamed at him, the front of her flame-coloured gown black where the drink had saturated it. 'Go — quick, before I bring Drew to deal with you!'

Pete shrugged, lunged into another table, saved it just in time, and then pursued an erratic course back to the bar.

'The dirty drunken tramp,' Val whispered, glaring after him.

'Yeah.' Dusty narrowed his eyes towards the bar, where Pete had just landed. 'I guess he saw what I had in my mind, too, though whether he was too pickled to know what it was or not I don't know.'

'Stay right here,' Val told him. 'I've got to change. I want to talk to you some more yet.'

Her fury was occasioned by far more than her ruined gown. She was inwardly convinced that the whole thing had been a trick specially arranged to discover what the old prospector was up to. This in turn meant her own information concerning the nugget might pass on elsewhere and so blow her own plans sky-high. She had been convinced that, given time, she could have got Dusty to speak. Now she was not so sure. Still flaming with anger she swung into her dressing-room and savagely ripped the costly gown from her body.

Meantime Pete was keeping up his act, using the counter for support and blearily surveying the saloon.

'Well?' Carson asked, round his cheroot.

'Gold,' Pete muttered. 'No doubt uv it, boss. He had a nugget on the table an' I knocked it to th' floor. Somehow the old critter's happened on the stuff somewheres.'

Carson turned lazily and picked up his drink, not showing by so much as a blink how suddenly excited he felt. A little distance away the Aztec girl was busy with her own drink also. She was beyond earshot of the two men, and in any case the noise in the saloon would have drowned Pete's whispered comments . . . but Maninza had her own ways of gathering information. She was an expert lip-reader.

Putting down her glass she tightened the kerchief a little at her throat and then set off towards the batwings.

'Good night, ma'am,' Carson said genially, touching his hat as she passed him.

'Good night, Mr Carson . . . ' Her voice was quiet, disarmingly smooth. It was queer somehow to hear a girl so educated in such a den. Even Valerie

Kent with her upbringing in a city was in no wise comparable to the enigmatic Aztec girl.

Carson watched her depart then turned to Pete again.

'Looks like the old fool has found a bonanza somewheres,' he said. 'And we want to know where it is. Leave him be for the moment, but when he quits follow him and take him up to my mountain shack. Mebbe I can persuade him to tell us a few things.'

'OK,' Pete acknowledged. 'I'll get the boys — '

'Do it later,' Carson snapped, gripping his arm. 'Don't let him have a single suspicion — And another thing, never let that Indian dame know there's a bonanza around here because it's probably hers by rights.'

Pete nodded. 'You got something there, boss. You mean that story of a lost mine which she's always looking for? Belongs to her ancestors, or sump'n?'

'That's it. She's searched every place

and not located it. Be just like that old fool Dusty Morgan to find it instead. We can deal with him, I reckon — but dealing with that Indian girl would be a different proposition. She's dangerous . . . Or anyways I think she is.'

'No doubt uv it,' Pete muttered — and returned his attention to watching Dusty. After a while he saw Val return in a sky blue gown and settle down to resume her conversation with him.

'OK,' Carson muttered. 'Get the boys together and wait outside. When Dusty appears y'know what to do with him. I'll join you at the shack later. Right now I'm goin' t'bust up this get-together between him and Val.'

Pete departed, not forgetting to maintain his unsteady gait, and Carson lounged across to where the girl and Dusty were absorbed in conversation.

'After what's happened you'd be safer telling me everything,' she insisted. 'You don't suppose that Pete was so greased he didn't know he'd gotten hold of a nugget, do you? When you step out of here you'll walk right into trouble. Let me have the facts and . . . '

Valerie stopped, aware of Carson's approach. He hadn't overheard anything so far and the girl was quite determined that he shouldn't.

'Reckon yore monopolizing my gal, old timer,' he said, genially enough. 'She an' me like to spend a bit of time together in an evening when she's finished her number.'

Dusty shrugged and buttoned up the collar of his shirt. Then he straightened his hat.

'OK, I can take a hint,' he said, getting up. 'Bin nice to see yuh again, Val — an' I'm hoping I'll see yuh some more afore I move on.'

'You're stayin' in town then?' Carson questioned.

'Yeah — figgered on doin'. Leastways fur a bit. I'll be seein' yuh.'

With a nod Dusty went on his way. He had one more drink at the bar and then headed for the batwings. Val watched him go, an intent look in her eyes. Carson saw her fingers clench before an inner thought.

'If yore thinkin' of following him, kid, forget it,' he said bluntly.

She gave him a quick, hurt look, startled at the way he had divined her intentions. He smiled blandly.

'Besides,' he added, 'the boys are a bit restive tonight. I guess an extra song wouldn't do 'em any harm.'

'But, Drew, I — '

'I said we could do with a song,' he repeated steadily, his dark eyes pinned on her. 'Better do it, kid.'

Angrily she turned to the piano, where the pianist was lounging and drinking beer. As she began singing she was conscious of only one thing — that she couldn't follow Dusty and, failing an effort to get the facts of the bonanza out of him, would not be a witness to whatever might happen to him, either.

There was a witness of another kind, however. Maninza, the Aztec girl, upon leaving The Last Frontier, had not followed her usual custom and ridden straight home. Instead she had only gone a little way along the high street, astride her pinto, then she had turned the animal, into the narrow space between two of the largest buildings. Now she sat motionless, her eyes watching the blaze of light at the front of the saloon, her own figure and that of the pinto hidden completely in the dense shadows away from the kerosene flares.

Maninza was prepared to wait as long as necessary: she had the infinite patience of her race, and much of its cruelty. There had been gold found, and the man who had found it, she gathered, was the dirty old prospector. Very well. Once he appeared outside the saloon she had her own plans for him —

But they did not mature. She saw him emerge, wiping the back of his hand over his mouth, and then descend the three steps to the tie-rack where his mule was tethered — but that was as far as he got. Just as she was about to hurtle her pinto out of concealment she reined in again suddenly as three horsemen sprang from the shadows to one side of the saloon. In a matter of seconds Dusty had been whipped up and was borne, shouting hoarsely, into darkness beyond the range of the kerosene lights.

Maninza waited a moment or two, then she nudged her pinto forward, across the street, and vanished in the darkness behind the buildings . . .

2

The moment Val came to the end of her song she gave one brief bow to acknowledge the honest-to-goodness clapping of the assembly and then went straight across to where Drew Carson was lounging against the bar. He eyed her as she came up. It was obvious from the hard glitter in her grey eyes and the set of her mouth that she was by no means in a good temper.

'I want a word with you, Drew!' she told him, and stood with hands on hips studying him.

'Sure,' he conceded lazily. 'Have a drink . . . '

'I don't want a drink; I want to talk. Let's go into your office.'

He shrugged, picked up his glass of whiskey to take it with him, then followed the girl's graceful figure across the saloon, up the small flight of stairs,

33

and so into his office which occupied a dominating position overlooking the entire main room.

'Now what?' Carson asked, lighting the lamp and then flinging down his hat. 'Have a seat.'

'I can say all I've got to say standing.' Val looked rather like a chicken in front of a bulldog. 'It's about Dusty.'

Carson grinned. 'I figgered it might be. Well, what about him?'

'That stunt with Pete was a trick, wasn't it? He wasn't drunk, or anywheres near it. He bumped into Dusty on purpose just to see what was going on.'

'Uh-huh. I sort of like to know what gives in my own saloon. I don't like private conversations — 'specially when yore the girl I've made up my mind to marry.'

'Don't be too sure of that, Drew!' Val snapped. 'To get back to the point, what are you going to do to Dusty?'

Carson drained his whiskey glass and then put it down on the roll-top.

'What do you care? No relation of yours, is he?'

34

'He happens to be a good friend — and if I know anything of you you'll not let him alone until he's talked.'

'About the gold nugget you mean?' And Val gave Carson a sharp look.

'Then I was right,' she decided. 'You know all about it.'

'Sure I do, kid. Dusty's found gold, and those sort of nuggets only come out of a bonanza. There are dozens of abandoned mines scattered around Arizona, I guess, all of 'em belonging to the original Aztecs. My guess is that Dusty's happened on one of 'em. Now what's the good of a fortune to an old *hombre* like him? Different with me. I can make good use of gold: make it pay for itself.'

'Until you sent Pete in upsetting everything I'd got a plan fixed to make Dusty talk,' Val said grimly. 'He blew it sky-high. Now I don't stand a chance with you at work as well.'

'What of it? When you marry me what I have is yours. You know that.'

'I'll never marry you, Drew, so get that through your head right now. I only stay at all because I can't find anything else. But you'll never get me — never. I wanted the details of Dusty's bonanza so I could buy myself out of this stinkhole you run. Now I've no chance.'

Carson looked at her steadily. Evidently thinking better of her earlier decision she now sat down and gave him a look of perplexity.

'Sorry, Val,' he said, 'but business is business. You should have more sense than to try and make plans which don't include me. I don't like women running business — leastways, not the gold business. My aim is to find out all I can from Dusty and then turn the information to account.'

'Suppose I went to work on him?' Val asked, thinking.

'Doing what? You don't suppose your curves'd make any impression on an old has-been like that, do you? Forget it, kid.'

'I've more ways of getting information than just relying on my figure!' Val retorted. 'What I mean is: if I could get

36

information from him, would you cut me in for fifty per cent of whatever we find in the bonanza?'

'No,' Carson replied flatly.

'Why not? I thought we were pretty close to each other.'

'So did I until you said just now that you'll never marry me. That washes things up between us, Val. If you hadn't said that I might have been sucker enough to fall for your fifty per cent line. As it is you do nothing, and get nothing. I'll work things my own way.'

Val's lips set tightly for a moment. She seemed to make up her mind and got to her feet.

'All right, Drew, if that's the way it is. You don't suppose I'm going to lie down and take it, though, do you?'

'No, my dear little chiseller, I don't. If ever a gal had her eye on the main chance, it's you — But steer clear of my affairs kid, or you may get hurt. An' I wouldn't like that. Beating up women doesn't come into my territory, unless I have to.'

'The way I look at it you've cheated me out of the chance of getting a gold mine,' Val said deliberately, 'and to get my chance back again I'm willing to go the limit.'

With that she left the office and slammed the door. Carson did not smile when she had gone. He lighted a cheroot and stood thinking. He had good reason to know that Val could, in an extremity, be a dangerous enemy. She was intelligent, resourceful, and just perched on the edge of being unscrupulous. It only needed a shove one way or the other to turn her into a ruthless hardbitten girl intent only on her own advancement — or into the unselfish, innocent young woman she had once been upon arrival in this lawless region. The thought of Val gone to the bad rather scared Carson. Men he could always handle, but women were different . . . Very.

And whilst he pondered possibilities Val collected her coat from her dressing-room and left the saloon. She boarded at the Mountain Hotel across the main street. Once in her own room she threw herself on the bed, fully dressed, and set herself to think. Something had to be done. An old man had a gold mine and it was far too good a prize for him to keep to himself.

Up to now she had no guarantee that Dusty had fallen foul of Drew Carson's boys, but she considered it pretty likely. There was a sure way to find out — He had said he was staying in town for a while. With the amount of gold dust he had with him — to say nothing of the nugget, though it was unlikely he would trade this for fear of giving too much away — he would be stopping either at this very hotel, or at Ma Gunthorpe's further down the street, the only two places where lodging was possible. So the answer seemed to be to make enquiry — and this Val did.

Fifteen minutes later she was back on the bed, thinking again. Dusty had not checked in at all, and nobody seemed to even be aware he was in town. After leaving The Last Frontier, he had apparently vanished — which was quite enough for Val. Slowly she formulated a plan, and though it meant bringing another into her private ambitions she considered it a good risk. By the time she was ready to retire properly she had made up her mind that a telegraph would be dispatched first thing in the morning . . .

It was also about this moment that Maninza, astride her pinto, urged the animal gently up a lonely arroyo in the mountain range, some three miles away from Hell's Acres. Her movements were completely hidden. The moon was not yet up and the glittering dust of stars did not give sufficient light for her darkclad figure to be picked out.

She was at the end of trailing Pete and his two cohorts from Hell's Acres. Having kept a constant distance from them she had followed them across pastureland, through the woody heart of juniper and cedar, and now to the higher reaches of the mountains where stood Drew Carson's shack. Log-walled, it was visible as a darker square against the uniform grey of the mountain walls. No light showed. Inside, the windows were covered with thick drapes.

Maninza was not prepared to act on the spur of the moment. For one thing she had only one gun with her — and to deal with three tough men she'd need two. For another she wanted to work out a plan to take the three men by surprise. She had the caution of her race, together with the hereditary ability to strike a swift and devastating blow when the moment was opportune. So for the time being she remained motionless, staring at the shack, the sweet-scented night breeze blowing in her immobile face.

After a while she dismounted. She knew that gold was the main reason for the prospector having been kidnapped — but whether it was just a few odd nuggets, which would be of no interest to her, or a genuine bonanza and therefore Aztec property, she did not know. But she could find out — if it were possible to overhear something . . .

Silently, close to the ground, like a tigress stalking her prey, she approached the shack, presently gaining its massive log walls. She drew her .32 from its holster just in case and then glided towards the nearest window. Using a boulder to give her an extra foot of height she straightened up and put her ear to the window's niche where it joined the frame. She found it difficult to hear the words beyond, particularly as the night wind made a perpetual swishing in the leaves of the cedar trees, but here and there snatches floated to her.

Inside the shack's main room Dusty was by this time roped to a chair, his wrists immovably knotted together behind him. In various parts of the room, where the glimmer of the single table oil-lamp hardly reached them, stood Pete and the two men who worked with him. As usual Pete was doing most of the talking, and enjoying it. Anything with a streak of sadism in it appealed to him.

'I guess the boss didn't tell me

exactly what I wus t'do with yuh, old timer,' he commented. 'I figger he wants t'go to work on yuh himself — but I can't see he'd mind much if I softened yuh up a bit in advance.'

The old prospector struggled futilely at the sound of the implacable voice behind him, but to budge the knots was useless. He could spit, though — and he did.

'That t'yuh!' he retorted. 'Y' can do what th' blue hell yuh like yuh low-down ornery cuss, but yuh won't git nothin' outa me. No, sir! If yuh kill me it won't make much odds. I'm an old buzzard now, anyways, an' I'd sooner die silent than live ter see jackals like you find my bonanza . . . '

Outside the window Maninza caught part of the old man's fierce words and stiffened intently.

'Stop talkin' like a fool, grandpa,' Pete responded sourly. He came round to face the tethered old man in the lamplight. 'That sorta talk don't get you no place. Yuh've only got to take us to th' bonanza an' frum then on yore free.'

'Yeah?' Dusty looked up at him fiercely. 'Expect me ter believe that? Yuh'd shoot me anyways, whether I showed yuh th' bonanza or not!'

Pete lost his temper. His right hand came round in a stinging slap on the old man's face and knocked him spinning, still tied to the chair. Impatiently Pete straightened the chair up again and stood looking down on the scowling prospector fiercely.

'If the boss gives me the OK, I'll make yuh wish yuh'd never been born,' he breathed. 'Until then yuh can sit right there, gettin' more cramped — without water an' without food . . . Al, Joe! Get these ropes tighter. Mebbe it'll help soften up the old fool.'

The remaining two men came forward and tightened the ropes to the limit; then from the kitchen they brought water and soaked the knots thoroughly. The old man said nothing but he knew he was in for hell when the ropes constricted even more about his

44

already tingling limbs . . .

For a time there was silence. Maninza made it the opportunity to glide away from the shack and return to her pinto. She was satisfied on two things — that Dusty Morgan really had found a bonanza, which was therefore her ancestral property; and also that he was too hard a nut to crack at the moment. Since he was obviously obdurate even before these three tough gunmen, there was no reason to assume he would be any the less obstinate if she herself could go to work on him — even though she did know one or two tricks of persuasion never heard of by a white man . . . Later, though, when his resistance was almost broken down. That would be the time.

She would watch — and wait . . .

★ ★ ★

The moment the telegraph office was open the following morning Val arrived and dispatched a long message to Rod

Gayland of the Double-8 ranch, situated some ten miles out of Hell's Acres. This done, she felt better and returned to her hotel. She thought little of the puncher whom she passed entering the telegraph office just as she was leaving it — but he thought plenty about her.

His actual mission was to buy tobacco, but he also went to the telegraph partition and spent a little while apparently making up his mind to send a message. Finally thinking better of it he tore off the top blank form, stuffed it in his pocket, and left.

A few minutes later he was in Drew Carson's office in The Last Frontier. The saloon owner had only just arrived and was looking through his morning mail, his feet on the desk, hat pushed up on his forehead. He slanted up his dark eyes as the puncher came in.

'What in hell d'you want?' he asked bluntly. 'Time you were up my spread lookin' after cattle, isn't it?'

'I wus on my way, boss — but I ran inter something. Thought you might like to know about it. Concerns Miss Kent.'

'Yeah? What about her?' Carson put his feet on the floor and his eyes were suspicious.

'Just this . . . ' The puncher took the blank telegraph form from his shirt pocket and tossed it on the desk. 'It struck me as queer that Miss Kent should need t'send a telegraph to anybody. I saw her through the glass of the door just before she left so I had a look at the form underneath the one she used. Yuh can faintly make out writing — '

'Yeah — Yeah, so you can,' Carson admitted, thinking; then he ran his finger round the inside of the oil-lamp chimney on the desk and began to apply the carbon in a fine dust into the indents of the blank form. By degrees the message the girl had written — rather too heavy-handedly — became vaguely decipherable . . .

ESSENTIAL YOU COME TO TOWN
STOP IMPORTANT NEWS FOR YOU

STOP MOUNTAIN HOTEL STOP VALERIE KENT.

'Kinda queer,' the puncher commented, stroking his chin. 'I can't make out the name it's sent to — 'less you can, boss.'

Carson went to work again with the lampblack and then took the smudgy form over to the window and examined it.

'Yeah — I can just get it,' he said at last. 'It's to Rod Gayland, of the Double-8.' He thought for a moment, crushing the form in his palm, then he shook his head. 'Can't say I'd know the guy if I saw him, though I've heard his name. He sure isn't a frequent visitor in town here.'

'What d'yuh s'pose Val Kent wants him fur?' the puncher demanded. 'It ain't as though she has any reg'lar truck with him — like yuh have yuhself f'r instance.'

'Whatever her object,' Carson said, turning, 'it isn't goin' to succeed. Grab off a couple of the boys from the spread and watch the trail from the Double-8.

48

When you see this guy comin' along it, headin' for town here, let him have it. And no mistakes! I don't like opposition.'

'OK,' the puncher agreed promptly, and left the office.

He had hardly gone and Carson had resumed his seat at the desk before Pete came in. He was looking irritated and as usual was badly in need of a shave. Carson gave him an enquiring look.

'Well, get anythin' outa that old buzzard yet?'

'No, boss — an' me an' th' boys are gettin' plenty sick of sittin' around in that shack uv yourn waitin' fur something to happen. I don't reckon that old critter'll ever speak. I never ran up against a guy so obstinate. He's worse than that durned mule uv his we had ter take along with us.'

'He'll talk,' Carson said calmly. 'Given time. You'll just have ter have patience.'

'Mebbe, but that ain't easy. Why in tarnation don't yuh come up to the shack an' give him the works yuhself?'

'Because I'm not wastin' my time. He'll crack after a while with no food or water and those ropes around him. Soon as he starts to, let me know.'

'Look, boss, it ain't no fun poked away up there,' Pete complained. 'If yuh'd only give me the say-so I could give it ter him neat — I'd blast it outa him, or kill him.'

'Yeah, that's what I'm afraid of,' Carson responded sourly. 'Kill him, and where'd we be? It isn't physical violence he needs but slow torture — and thirst in a region like this can be a mighty tough persuader. He'll start talkin' when he's burnin' up — Meantime git back to the shack and stop there. Only report when yuh have to. Pick yourself up some food on the way.'

'I'm not stayin' in that dump indefinitely!' Pete snapped. 'All three uv us need a relief party ter take over.'

'You'll get it, soon as I can fix it. I've two of the boys doing another job at the moment. Now stop belly-aching and get out!'

Pete went, doing his best to disguise the resentment he felt at being shut away from town with only his two comrades and a tight-lipped old man for company . . . Carson sat thinking for a time after his gunhawk's departure, debating as to whether he had made the right move in detailing three of his men to take care of Rod Gayland.

Finally he decided that he had acted wisely. To shoot Rod Gayland as he came down-trail to Hell's Acres would be easy enough, and there wouldn't be any evidence to show who had done it. There had been the other alternative of intercepting the telegraph rider from Arrowhead as he brought the message out to the Double-8 — Arrowhead being only two miles from Rod Gayland's ranch, a town smaller than Hell's Acres but possessing its own telegraph station none the less. Intercepting a Government rider was dangerous business, however, and Carson was not prepared to get mixed up in it.

He lighted a cheroot, satisfied in his

own mind that everything would work out just as he had planned it — and perhaps it would have done but for trouble with a horseshoe.

When the telegraph was delivered Rod Gayland was busy re-fitting a shoe to his sorrel assisted at the forge by his side-kick and ranch foreman Bill Tandrill. Bill — blubbery, none too intelligent, but as willing as a horse — continued with the shoeing as Rod read the telegraph through twice. Then he frowned and cuffed his black sombrero up on his sweating forehead.

'Must be something mighty important,' he commented at length.

'Yeah?' Bill Tandrill looked up enquiringly from the stench of burning horn. 'What gives, Rod?'

Rod read the message aloud and Bill Tandrill listened attentively; then be tossed the still ill-fitting horseshoe back in the forge embers and worked the bellows-handle up and down.

'Val?' he repeated, rubbing his chins. 'Don't recollect seein' her any place.'

'You haven't,' Rod grinned. 'I've only seen her twice myself, but it was for long enough to get acquainted. She'd just arrived in Hell's Acres at that time and she struck me as bein' too nice a girl for a hell-hole like that, and I told her so. Haven't seen her since, though I've thought about her plenty . . . From the look of this telegraph she's been thinking about me, too.'

'You mean you kinda fell for her?' Bill asked drily.

'Mebbe — but I'm not the type to push things. I thought I'd let her get settled down a bit before looking her up — Now it seems I'm going to do it quicker than I figgered. I can't imagine what she can have to say to me but I'll sure have to go and find out.'

'Uh-huh,' Bill agreed, and eyed the red-hot horseshoe critically. 'Want me with you?'

Rod considered this. Then he gave a nod. 'Perhaps be as well. Hell's Acres is no place for a stranger — especially if he isn't particularly welcome, which I somehow feel I shan't be from the sound of this telegraph. Only one man in Hell's Acres who counts, remember, and that's Drew Carson of The Last Frontier. I guess Val must be pretty friendly with him otherwise she wouldn't still be in Hell's Acres. With him on her side she's safe — Yeah, I reckon you'd better come too. Be safer.'

'This horse of yourn isn't going to be ready for an hour,' Bill decided, setting to work to hammer the shoe. 'Not if I'm to make a proper job of it. You'd better take my mare and I'll come on later with the sorrel here.'

'OK.' Rod began moving lithely towards his ranch-house. 'I'll tell the boys to carry on as usual until I get back: which with so many cattle deals coming up I hope won't be long.'

'Say — wait a minute, Rod — ' Bill came hurrying after him, the glowing shoe in the tongs. 'S'pose you're longer than you figger? Where'll you be stayin'?'

'Ma Gunthorpe's,' Rod told him, and

went up steps of the ranch-house porch.

He delayed only long enough to have a shave, change into a clean shirt and pants, and strap on cross-over holsters — then he went out and saddled the mare and set off on his journey . . . Nor did he take the direct trail route. There was short cut across the pasturelands which he used if ever he visited Hell's Acres, a cut which took him through a good deal of woodland country which more or less made cover for his trip. Not that he had the least suspicion anything would really happen to him, but precaution was inbred in him in this land of lawless men who had a gun handy for everything.

On the main trail, high atop a rimrock and well shielded, the three gunhawks whom Carson had detailed to get Rod Gayland kept an alert watch-out — but saw nothing . . . until a lone figure at last began to appear from the distance, his presence first revealed by a plume of dust in the blinding sunlight.

'He's comin'!' one of the men breathed, watching intently from under his lowered hat brim. 'What do we do? — go down and pop him off as he passes?'

'Yeah — lets' go.' It was the puncher who had brought Carson the telegraph form who gave the order. He swung into the saddle of his horse and led it down the sleeply shelving cliff face until the road level was reached; then he drew into the concealment of a tall rock spur and looked at his two companions.

'Kerchief your faces,' he ordered, drawing up his own to his eyes. 'We don't want the guy to know who we are just in case our shots don't go true an' he only gets winged . . . I'll shoot first. If he keeps goin' you follow through with your own hardware — OK, here he comes!'

The gunhawk eased his heavy .45 into his right hand and rested the barrel in a niche in the rock. He waited until the rider came into range — then he fired. With the explosion the rider crashed sideways from his saddle into the dust. The sorrel cantered a few yards, startled, then veered off into the grass bordering the trail and came to a standstill, whinnying.

'OK,' the puncher muttered, as the figure remained motionless. 'I guess that got him.'

'Better check up,' one of the others said.

'I don't aim to take that risk. If he's only lying doggo he could pull a gun on the lot uv us afore we could get to him — He's slugged all right, and that's all we came fur. Now let's get outa here.'

He remounted his horse, spurred it fiercely, and with his two companions hit the trail for Hell's Acres. When the noise of their hoofbeats had died away Bill Tandrill raised his head cautiously and looked about him.

'Nice greeting for a feller,' he muttered, and tugged off his Stetson. Then as he examined it he whistled. A hole had been drilled clean through it barely half an inch above the point where the top of his skull came. He had instinctively flung himself to the trail at the sound of the shot — an old trick — and lain there until he had seen what was to happen next. The split second between the explosion and the arrival of the bullet, and his movement therein, had left him unscathed, but decidedly worried.

'Wonder if they got Rod?' he mused; then deciding there was only one way to find out he retrieved the sorrel from the nearby field, mounted it and hit leather again for Hell's Acres.

At this particular moment Rod was riding into town. Gaining the main street he reduced his mare's pace to a jog-trot and looked about him. The boardwalks were busy; buckboards and teams were moving up and down the high street. Here and there a curious glance was cast at the tall young man with the square shoulders and determined chin, his white sombrero pushed back on to his blond hair. There was something different about him, marking him out from the usual run of punchers and saddle tramps who frequented the ramshackle town. Since he had only visited the place three times in his life — Arrowhead being his chief source of supply — he was a virtual stranger.

He kept on riding until he reached the Mountain Hotel. Leaving his mare at the tie-rack he entered the main hall of the building and in a few more minutes was knocking on the door of the girl's room on the first floor.

She admitted him immediately, having seen his arrival. He gave her a curious glance as he saw the anxiety on her face.

'Howdy, Val,' he greeted, taking off his sombrero and shaking hands. 'What's on your mind?'

'Plenty — and it was decent of you to come considering we're not very closely acquainted.'

'Think nothing of it. Glad to have the chance.'

Val said nothing as she motioned to chairs. For some reason she felt awkward in the presence of this big,

59

clean-limbed young giant with the genial smile. It made her feel hypersensitive concerning her own hard-bitten streak. There was something so downright noble about him he unconsciously made her feel uncomfortable.

'What's this about important news?' he asked. 'Important to you, or to me?'

'To both of us. It concerns a bonanza, and it's gotten so far out of hand I just can't control it. When you know that Drew Carson is mixed up in it you'll realise why . . . '

Rod nodded, his steady blue eyes on the girl's face. She told him the whole story of the old prospector, of how she suspected he had been kidnapped, and of the possibility of him knowing of the whereabouts of a gold mine.

'My idea is for you to try and help me locate Dusty,' she explained. 'I'm no good whatever when it comes to tracking — but you are used to this region and might manage something. If we can only find Dusty and get him out of Carson's clutches I've a feeling

Dusty might reward us with information about his mine.'

'Mebbe,' Rod said, but did not look too convinced. 'Or have you another reason?'

The girl looked surprised. 'Such as?'

'Well, from what you tell me Drew Carson has handed you a pretty raw deal. You might have found out plenty from this prospector if Carson hadn't queered things. Seems to me this set-up smells more of you wanting to be revenged on Carson than anything else. The mine, I get the feeling, is only a kind of secondary consideration with you.'

'Well . . . perhaps you're right,' Val admitted, shunning his keen look. 'Only natural I should want to get my own back, isn't it? If I were a man I'd shoot it out with Carson and try and find the old man — But I'm not. That's why I thought you might like to help me. If you don't want to there's nothing to stop you riding straight back to the Double-8.'

Rod grinned. 'Hold your horses, Val.

I'm not going back now I've gotten this far. You know I'd do a favour for you anytime. Just that I'm a bit surprised to find you have a vengeful streak, that's all. I'd never have suspected it, from our earlier acquaintance.'

'Time's changed me,' she excused herself.

'Mebbe — an' it doesn't suit you.' Rod got to his feet, thumbs latched into his cross-over belts. 'Just the same I'm not the kind of guy to let an old man be at the mercy of gunhawks if I can help it. I'll try and find him if only to free him — if he wants to talk about gold afterwards, OK, that's his privilege. First, though, let me get something straight. How much does Drew Carson know of your present moves?'

'Not a thing. He knows I was furious at the way he'd broken up my plans, but beyond that doesn't think I can do anything. And he doesn't know you, either — far as I know. That was what made me think of you. You can act with freedom. All I've got to do is pretend not to know you, and that makes you a stranger in town able to do as you like.'

'Mmmm, guess you're right,' Rod admitted. 'No, Carson doesn't know me, unless he may have glimpsed me by sight when I was last in town here. And he doesn't know Bill Tandrill, either. He'll be along shortly to join me.'

'Bill Tandrill?' Val questioned.

'My best friend — and foreman of my spread. Handy guy to have around. Shoots straight and doesn't ask too many questions.' Rod strolled to the window and without revealing himself too plainly studied the street and The Last Frontier opposite.

'Carson still runs the saloon,' Val said, joining him. 'And the town too, pretty well.'

'Including you,' Rod remarked drily. 'Pity. You're too nice a girl for that. Or were . . .'

'Have I changed that much?' she asked, her eyes serious.

'Mebbe I notice it more not having seen you in some time. I guess you're not quite the Val I knew earlier — but mebbe you will be now we've met up again. You don't want to let the gun-hawks of this town bend you to their way of thinking, Val, not when you're made of better stuff . . . ' He paused.

'Anyway,' Rod continued, changing the subject, 'the saloon seems to have opened for the day so I can't do better than go over and size up Drew Carson for myself. Maybe I'll figger a way to trick him into saying something unwary. If that fails I'll have to see if I can't do a bit of tracking on my own account. Fact remains that Dusty Morgan has to be found. I suppose I shan't see you there across the road?'

'Not until evening — then I'm on duty until closing time. Being a hostess in that dive can get pretty vile, too.'

'I can imagine,' Rod sympathized. 'Anyways, probably it's as well for you to be absent, then you won't have any chance to give away the fact that you know me . . . That much settled, I'll be on my way.'

He shook the girl's hand again, gave her an encouraging smile, and stepped out into the passage way. From the window of her room she secretly watched him cross the road, leading his mare. She felt that his arrival had taken her back quite a few months to the time when she had arrived unspoiled in this ramshackle town of corruption and gun dictatorship . . .

3

Drew Carson was at his accustomed place beside the bar when Rod Gayland walked in. At this hour of the day customers were few — there were no more than half a dozen sprinkled at the many tables. It was in the evening when Carson did all the business, and swelled his considerable bank account.

He stood watching the crisply dressed young man as he advanced, impressed by his easy strength and good appearance.

'Howdy,' he greeted, as Rod stopped at the counter and ordered a rye.

Rod returned the salutation with a nod, then looked about him.

'Seen any sign of a fat chap in a black Stetson around here?' he questioned.

'Guess I haven't, stranger. Nobody else been in 'cept those you see at the tables. If yore in a hurry I can give him

66

a message if he looks in.'

'No hurry,' Rod said, shrugging, and swallowed part of his drink. 'Thanks just the same.'

Silence. Drew Carson's cheroot smouldered. There was a clink of glasses as the barkeep cleaned up.

'Passing through?' Carson asked presently. 'Guess I don't remember seein' you around these parts before.'

'Some time since I was last here,' Rod told him. 'Mebbe I'll stay a few days; Mebbe not. Haven't figured it out yet.'

'Uh-huh.' Carson was tempted to ask Rod his name outright, then instead he glanced up as the batwings swung before the arrival of three punchers. Immediately Carson moved towards them and drew them to a corner.

'We plugged him, boss,' the leader murmured, with a quick glance round the saloon. 'Just as he wus a-comin down the trail. Guess you shouldn't be troubled by him no more.'

'Good enough,' Carson acknowledged. 'For your own sakes I hope you made a good job of it. OK, guess yore entitled to a drink. Go help yourselves.'

He followed them across the saloon back to the bar and resumed his former lounging position. One or two customers came in and settled at the tables. Rod finished his drink and then stood for a moment contemplating the three punchers who were looking at him curiously.

'Interested, fellers?' he asked briefly.

They started, then returned their attention to their drinks. Carson gave them an ugly look.

'Ain't you got no more damned sense than to stare at a stranger when he walks into town?' he demanded. And to Rod he added, 'I guess I should apologize for 'em. Can't expect much else from a bunch of cattle-shifters.'

'I've been looked at before,' Rod said drily, rolling himself a cigarette. 'An' say, there's a question I'd like to ask you.'

'Sure thing — anything you like. I know most things around here. Carson's the name — Drew Carson. I own this joint.'

Carson meant it as an invitation for Rod to supply his own name, but he sidestepped the issue and asked a question instead.

'What are the prospects of finding gold around here?'

The three punchers in the background put down their glasses and listened intently. Carson went on smoking, his eyes narrowed a trifle.

'Same as they are anywheres in Arizona, I reckon. Why?'

'Oh . . . ' Rod shrugged. 'I'm a mining engineer and I just figgered I might do myself some good if there was any chance of locating gold around these parts. I hear stories, you know, and I did think there was one particular mine around these parts which is rightfully owned by the Aztecs.'

'Yeah, sure there is,' Carson admitted. 'The story's pretty well circulated, I guess — and there's one Aztec in particular who would like to find the mine you're talking about. A woman by the name of Maninza. She — '

Rod looked up in surprise as Carson stopped; then he followed his gaze towards the batwings. The big, lumbering figure of Bill Tandrill had just entered. He was covered in trail dust, his hat on the back of his head. It was not so much Bill's entry that had checked Carson as the gasp that had come from the three punchers behind him.

'Sweet hell!' the leading puncher exploded. 'It's him!'

Carson twirled. 'Who?'

'Rod Gayland, boss! I thought we'd rubbed him out — '

Though he did not quite understand the set-up Rod's hand blurred to his right Colt and whipped it from the holster. Bill Tandrill paused for a moment, frowning, then he came forward.

'Look, Rod, what gives?' he demanded. 'I couldn't find you at the hotel so I came on here . . . '

Carson's eyes went wider as he looked at Rod, then down at the shining barrel of the Colt. Rod's eyes were steady, pinning him.

'What's the explanation, Carson?' he asked, his voice taut.

'Set-up's plain enough,' Bill Tandrill said, reaching the bar and ordering a whiskey. 'Some guy shot at me as I came along the trail and gave my hat some ventilation — ' He held it up for inspection. 'I laid doggo until the coast was clear and then came on here.'

'In other words you were mistaken for me,' Rod said.

Carson's face became more deeply tanned as he eyed the three startled punchers.

'You blasted boneheads, why couldn't you — '

'I'll do the talking, Carson,' Rod interrupted. 'How did you know I was coming, anyway? Who told you?'

Carson's mouth set in an ugly line and he said nothing. For a second there was a grim silence — then Rod jerked his head back with a gasping cry as whiskey, hurled from the glass of the puncher behind the saloon owner, swamped into his face and eyes. A split second after it a hammer blow to the jaw knocked him sprawling to the saw-dust, his gun flying out of his hand.

'If we didn't take care of him before there ain't no reason why we can't now,' the puncher grated, his gun in his hand. 'I don't aim to make a mistake twice . . . '

He fired, but at the identical moment Carson slammed up his arm. The bullet whanged into the ceiling.

'You gun-crazy fool!' Carson yelled. 'Do you think I want a murder on my hands right in my own saloon . . . ?'

He got no further. Bill Tandrill, who had taken a second or two to size things up, slammed out a right that sent bursting fire through Carson's head. He slithered backwards, clutching at the bar for support blood streaming from his nose. Tandrill, for all his blubber, had cast-iron muscles beneath it.

The nearest puncher twisted round Carson and dived for Rod's fallen gun, but before he reached it Bill Tandrill's boot shot out and cracked the puncher violently under the chin. With a howl of pain he fell back, nursing his jaw.

'I get the idea we're not so welcome around here,' Bill said, as Rod scrambled to his feet, his fallen gun back in his hand. 'What's the answer, Rod? Shoot the jiggers?'

Rod shook his head quickly. 'I guess not. I'm no killer.' He gave a quick glance round the saloon where the few customers were watching the proceedings with profound interest. 'Guess the best thing we can do is get out. There are four of 'em to two of us: opposition's too tough. I'll be back, Carson,' he added, 'and in the meantime here's a souvenir . . .'

He holstered his gun and lashed up his fist in a blinding uppercut all in one movement. Carson took it well and truly on the jaw and crashed over on to his back, bringing down a rain of bottles and glasses on top of him. By the time his dazed senses had recovered a little and his three gunhawks had hauled him up Rod and Bill Tandrill had vanished.

'You idiots!' Carson breathed hard and rubbed his aching face. 'You blasted, bird-brained dopes — ! Not only did you get the wrong man — an' miss him! — but that damned gunplay of yours has made it clear to Rod Gayland that we're on the prod for him.'

'Look, boss, we . . . '

'Get out!' Carson yelled.

So the three men got out, as fast as they could go. Carson fingered his aching face again and then turned to the barkeep to demand a drink. He swallowed it, began to feel better, and lit a fresh cheroot.

'So that's her game,' he muttered, scowling. 'She reckons that that fancy rancher can muscle in and mebbe upset my plans. Guess that gal needs taking care of, but fast.'

For a moment his fury urged him to go there and then to the girl's hotel and deal with her — then reflection decided him to wait. For one thing he might not get away with it in the hotel with other

74

boarders around: for another thing a girl who had been beaten up would be too much of a spectacle by daylight. Later on she would be coming to The Last Frontier anyway to perform her usual duties. Then — Carson nodded to himself, satisfied.

Then he began to think further. All his worries could be resolved in one sweep if that obdurate old fool of a prospector could only be made to talk. Making up his mind he left the saloon and went down the steps to his horse at the tie-rail, In a few moments he had mounted it and began to ride swiftly out of town, presently striking the trail which led to Paradise Mountains.

He was so lost in his own grim thoughts it came as an absolute surprise to him when, as he was about to enter the woodland at the mountain foothills, he became aware of a rider on each side of him, their guns levelled.

'Just keep riding, Carson,' Rod said grimly. 'It'll be healthier. Thanks for starting on the move so soon.'

Carson kept riding because he could do nothing else. He glared in fury.

'Where in hell did you two critters spring from?' he snapped.

'Nothing magical about it,' Rod told him. 'You don't suppose we went very far when we left the saloon, do you? We decided to stick around and see if you or any of your boys went on a ride out of town — perhaps to wherever you've got Dusty Morgan hidden. It happened to be you — an' we followed. So keep going.'

'You know all about Morgan then?' Carson demanded.

'Sure thing. Not as much as I'd like to, though. You're going to take us straight to him, Carson, and if you don't it'll be just too bad.'

'That goes for me too,' Bill Tandrill affirmed, his gun steadily aimed.

Carson knew perfectly well that he was in a tough spot, but since his shack was still some miles ahead there was time yet in which to think and perhaps pull some trick. To escape he would have to use his own resources. If the shack was reached Pete and the boys would see what had happened, certainly, but they would be unlikely to fire for fear of hitting their boss — so whatever move was made it had to be quick, and certain.

'Talkative, ain't he?' Bill Tandrill remarked drily, as the journey through the woodland with its dapplings of sunlight continued.

Rod said nothing. His gun was ready; his eyes were watching Carson keenly. He was prepared for any trick the saloon owner might pull — except the one he *did* pull. It happened as they were passing under the low branch of a tree.

Carson was between Rod and Bill Tandrill and, though covered by the guns, his hands were free. Abruptly he flung his hands up, gripped the tree branch, and drew himself from the saddle. In those few seconds Rod and Bill moved on perhaps a yard — which was just what Carson wanted. Still gripping the branch he lashed forward both his heavy-shod feet, striking each man in the back violently. The thing was done so suddenly and painfully they had no chance to grasp what had happened. By the time they had twisted round, their spines throbbing, Carson had dropped to the dense undergrowth and had his guns levelled.

'All right,' he said sourly. 'Throw down your hardware and then follow it.'

There was nothing else for it. Rod and Bill both dropped their guns — which Carson collected and stuck in his belt — then they slid from their saddles and kept their hands up. He took their remaining guns and considered the two men cynically.

'Smart, ain't you?' he asked. 'Since it seems you want to fight it out with me, Gayland, you might as well start in right now. This is the first round — and I won it, see.'

'You're a long time putting bullets into us, ain't you?' Bill asked.

'I don't aim to shoot you, that's why.

Bullets can be traced to the guns they come from and I've a nosy sheriff to think of. I've better methods. Go an' stand by that low tree branch there!'

Both men looked at each other, then obeyed. Though there were two of them they knew better than to try and tackle as good a gunman as Carson, alert as he was for every move . . . Still keeping them covered he went to his horse and took a lariat from the saddlehorn. Working one handedly he cut the rope into two sections with his hunting-knife, using slip knots to fasten the hands of both men securely, behind them. This done he was able to move more easily.

With their own lariats he noosed their necks, carrying the rope up to the low branch of the tree under which they were standing. They remained watching and wondering — then gradually they saw the ingenuity, and fiendishness, of Carson's plan.

By main strength he bent down the springy branch until its further end almost touched the ground. Here he anchored it with a remaining piece of lariat to a nearby tree-trunk. He spent some moments taking up the slack in the ropes about the men's necks and making the knots secure to the branch — then he set to work to carefully cut the strands of the tension-rope until only two remained.

'Guess that does it,' he said finally. 'An old trick but a nice one — and leaves no traces. Your blasted necks are fastened to this branch, and at the moment you're OK. But I've frayed the cord holding the branch down. It won't stand the upward strain for more than ten minutes — In fact it's unravelling right now. When it snaps the branch will shoot back where it was — and you'll go with it. Necktie party, see? — with nobody present as witnesses. No clue, no nothing. Guess that should take care of you boys, nicely.'

Carson grinned widely at the stony looks he got, then he turned to his horse, taking the sorrel and mare with him, and continued on his way through the wood. At length he was lost to sight and the sound of vegetation being trampled by the horses died away.

'Nice mess to be in,' Bill Tandrill said bitterly, making a futile effort to shift the cords which bound his wrists. 'We oughta have been more careful in watching that jigger, Rod.'

'We will be . . . next time.' Rod looked about him anxiously, casting in his mind for some way of escape.

'Next time? There isn't goin' to be one unless I miss my guess — Look at that rope! Y'can see it unravelling even as you watch it.'

Rod turned his attention to it, setting his mouth as he saw the hairlike threads bending and twisting into view as the cord slowly gave way under the tremendous strain pulling at it — Then at a sudden sound from behind them both men looked up quickly and turned as far as they dared.

To their surpise a young woman in a scarlet blouse and black riding pants was visible. She dismounted quickly from her pinto and came forward, the twilight glancing on to the ebony of her hair and deepening the red of her skin.

Without uttering a word she slashed through the ropes which were fastened to the branch from the men's necks — then with one sweep of the blade she cut the cord holding down the branch itself. It lashed back into position with a swift crepitation of breaking leaves.

'Say, miss, we're mighty grateful to you,' Rod said urgently, as she turned to face him. 'We were in a tough spot.'

'Yes; I could see that.' She smiled a little and revealed perfect teeth. Then she slipped her knife back in her belt.

'You're an Aztec, ain't you?' Bill asked, over Rod's shoulder.

'I am — and proud of it.' She looked at him steadily with her dark eyes. 'My name is Maninza.'

'Fortunate you happened to be around,' Rod said; then with a frown he added, 'Quite a coincidence, in fact. There can't be many people come this way.'

'There was no coincidence about it,' the girl said, shrugging. 'I have been keeping a watch on Drew Carson for quite some time, so my seeing what he had done to you was purely because I was following him. I have my own reasons for keeping track of him. I didn't release you because I have any particular regard for you — indeed I have no regard for the white race at all — but because you are obviously enemies of Carson. Since I am also, that places you both on my side.'

'Uh-huh, I suppose it does,' Rod agreed, still looking puzzled. 'We've a score to settle with Carson — My name's Rod Gayland. This is my ranch foreman, Bill Tandrill.'

Maninza nodded but did not say anything.

'What happens now, then?' Bill asked. 'Do you want us to do something for you? If so we will, willingly, after what you have done for us.'

'I am not in need of assistance, thank you,' the Aztec girl said politely. 'I know perfectly well how to conduct my own affairs, and I leave you to conduct yours. You are free to deal with Drew Carson as you wish — unless I happen to deal with him first.'

She turned to go, but Rod caught her arm.

'A moment, Miss Maninza. You said something a moment ago about us being on your side. Wouldn't it be as well if I knew what you intend doing? What's your grudge against Drew Carson?'

'No grudge, Mr Gayland. He just happens to be in the way of certain plans I've made.'

'Could they be connected with . . . gold, and a kidnapped prospector?'

Maninza looked at Rod steadily for a moment, but she did not answer the question. Instead she jerked her arm away from his grip and returned to her pinto. Without so much as a backward glance she mounted it and rode off quickly into the heart of the woodland.

Bill came clumping forward, his hat

pushed up on his forehead.

'Wimmin!' he muttered. 'I never could figure 'em. An' I can figger that one least of all. What I know of Redskins they usually leave the whites in a spot if they can: instead of that she freed us.'

'With an end in view,' Rod told him quietly. 'To her way of thinking we are better alive to assist — even if remotely — in the downfall of Carson, than hanging on a tree with our necks stretched. No Redskin ever did anything for a white, Bill, unless it was to benefit the Redskin.'

'Yeah — mebbe you got something there . . . Well, what happens now? Try and pick up Carson's trail and follow him? He's probably gone to the shack.'

'There's no doubt of it — but what do you suppose we could do there? For one thing we've no guns and for another we've no horses. We can't attempt anything until we're re-equipped. Best thing we can do is return to Hell's Acres while we know Carson is out of the way, buy a couple of guns and hire two horses;

then we'll think further. Later on we'll deal with Carson properly, and probably get our hardware and cayuses back again.'

'OK,' Bill agreed, and turned to begin the journey — then he paused as Rod did not move with him. He was thinking something out, and presently it took the form of words.

'It occurs to me,' Rod said, 'that Val is going to be in a mighty dangerous position from here on. Carson will soon put two and two together and tumble to it that she sent for me — and when that happens he's likely to make things hot for her. We'll have to keep on the watch. We'll also trail Carson, or one of his boys, next time any of them set out for the shack — Pity is we showed ourselves this time, otherwise we'd have been well away. Over-confident, I guess!'

'Could be,' Bill agreed. 'Anyways, let's get back into town. I'm getting cold without my hardware . . . '

*   *   *

Drew Carson did not return to The Last Frontier until nightfall, and he was in a livid temper. All day long, since arriving at the shack, he had tried every method of persuasion he could think of to make Dusty Morgan speak — without result . . . By this time the old man, bruised and battered from beatings-up, worn out from lack of water, food, and rest, was pretty nearly at the end of his tether — a fact of which Maninza was fully aware — but he still had enough obstinacy left to deny the gunhawks the information they wanted.

Carson's temper had not been improved, either, by the discovery — on his return through the woodland — that Rod Gayland and Bill Tandrill were not hanging dead on a tree branch as he had planned. He had found the cut ropes — and nothing more. Which meant he was in the grip of a profound uncertainty, not knowing what had happened to the two men who would now obviously be hell-bent on getting him.

Smouldering, dirty and tired from his activities, he entered his saloon — leaving his own horse and the appropriated mare and sorrel outside at the tie-rack — and went straight through to his office. Val, in the midst of one of her songs, saw him arrive and caught the glare he gave her. She felt her heart beat a little faster when one of the waiters came over to tell her that Carson wanted her in his office immediately.

She found him slumped before his desk, busy with a whiskey bottle. His eyes glinted as she came in. Getting up he walked past her and shot the bolt into place on the door.

'Something the matter?' she asked, hesitating.

'Plenty.' His eyes pinned her. 'I suppose the notion of bringing Rod Gayland here was to get your own back on me for spoiling your chances with Dusty Morgan?'

'How do you know about Rod?' Val demanded, her mouth setting.

'Your dear little boyfriend didn't rat

on you, Val, if that's what you're thinking — It so happens one of my men saw you send off a telegram, and by a little strategy I found out what message you'd sent. I tried to get Gayland rubbed out — and failed. Now he's God knows where, waitin' for me — Thanks to you I'm in danger of my life.'

Val smiled cynically. 'Nice to hear you admit it.'

'Yeah? Try laughing this one off — ' Carson's hand swung round and struck her violently across the face. She jerked back her head, her cheek flaming.

'Time's come to break my rule about women,' Carson explained, his mouth twisted. 'If ever there's a low-down cheater in the female species, it's you! There ain't a woman breathing, Val, who can try crossing me — '

He swung, snatched down the big horsewhip from behind the door, and then slashed it round with all his strength. Drink, frustration, plain cruelty — all three drove into a murderous attack. Val stood no chance against it though she struggled to save herself behind the furniture. Carson's flailing arm seemed to be everywhere and Val's world a white-hot sea through which she stumbled and reeled blindly. Until at last the onslaught ceased. Numb with pain she remained motionless, face down on the dusty carpet. Far away she heard the rattle of the whip being flung on one side and then Carson's grating, breathless voice.

'Mebbe that'll teach you to keep outa my plans! Now yore gettin' outa town, Val — and yore stopping out too if you know what's good for yuh. I'll take you half way to Arrowhead and you can finish the journey as best you can — Get on your feet!'

As she did not move he stooped and lifted her in his powerful arms. She stirred a little.

'An' yore sure not going through my place in this state,' he added. 'Be just what you'd like t'do, wouldn't it? — advertise what I've done to you and try to get some sympathy. Well, it ain't going to work.'

He supported her with one arm for a moment and with his free hand opened the office window. It looked out on to the narrow veranda which extended from the back of the building. Clutching the girl tightly he slid with her down the roof, released her, and jumped down. Then he hauled her down after him and carried her swiftly to the front of the building. Before moving on to the three mounts still fastened to the tie-rack he cast a cautious glance about him, but at the moment the main street was practically deserted — enough for him to risk moving, anyway.

In a matter of seconds he had put the half fainting girl into the saddle of Rod's mare; then he jumped quickly to his own horse. Reaching across, he supported the girl with one hand as he urged both animals out of the high street, and then the town, as fast as he could go. He began to breathe more freely as the kerosene flares were replaced by the steady glitter of the stars and he had the emptiness of the trail before him.

The rushing of the night wind past her face revived Val somewhat, but she realized there was just nothing she could do. She was unarmed and entirely at Carson's mercy. If he chose to kill her — though as far as she could remember he had not said he would — that would be the end of it, and as she felt at the moment she did not particularly care if he did.

Apparently he had no such intention. When they had been riding for half an hour and the trail had resolved itself into a narrow white line skirting the edge of the desert, he drew his horse to a halt and dragged on the mare's reins to slow it down.

'Yore on your own from here, Val,' he said briefly. 'Keep going to Arrowhead and from there on go where the hell you like. Show your face in Hell's Acres again and I'll kill you — so get that through your skull. Since you wanted to play rough you can't blame me for beatin' the tar outa you.'

With that he swung away and set his

mount speeding into the night. Val listened to the receding hoof-beats, then, still feeling dizzy, she tumbled from the saddle and sat down wearily in the grass to try and recover something of her strength. From head to foot she was aching and her back smarted viciously where the whip tails had cut through her frock and into her flesh. Just how she looked she did not dare to think.

It was the sound of approaching riders which presently roused her from her lethargy. Her first instinct was to hide herself in the vegetation at the side of the trail — but there just was not time. The two horsemen were upon her in the starlight before her aching limbs could move her, then a long sigh escaped her as she recognized the voice of Rod.

'Val, what's been happening to you? You hurt?'

He came speeding across from his horse and put his arm about her shoulders. She winced and gave a little moan of pain at the sudden pressure on her cut flesh.

'What goes on?' he asked grimly, relaxing his hold. 'Carson been busy?'

'I-I guess so, Rod. He-he found out that it was I who sent for you and he went berserk. He got me in his office and laid into me with a horsewhip.'

'I see.' Rod's voice was like steel and he glanced up at Bill Tandrill's bulky figure as he kneeled in the starlight and looked down at the girl.

'How did you find me?' Val asked.

'We saw Carson bring you out of his saloon. We've been on the watch for him. He got away so fast there was no time then to intercept him, so we followed. We could have dealt with him when we saw him ride back along the trail — but instead we kept out of sight and then came on to find you, figuring you might need more attention than him. We could tell when he brought you out of the saloon that you were in a fainting condition.'

'I've the feeling,' Bill said slowly, 'that Carson is going to pay an account for this bit of work. Look at her back! Her

94

frock's cut to pieces, and streaks of blood are — '

'Shut up,' Rod interrupted flatly. 'Don't need to make it any worse for her than it is, do you?' He slipped his big hands under the girl's armpits and raised her easily to a standing position. 'OK,' he said, 'you're going back into town where you can be taken care of.'

'But I daren't, Rod!' she protested. 'Drew warned me that if I went back to Hell's Acres he'd kill me.'

'He won't be in any fit state to kill anybody by the time I've finished with him. Trust me; I know what I'm doing.'

'I-I don't quite understand what's been happening,' Val said, confused. 'Where have you been and what have you done since you left me at the hotel this morning?'

'I've done plenty. We both have — Bill Tandrill here, and I. Now we're going to do plenty more — '

'And what about Dusty? Did you find him?'

'Not yet. Right now your safety is

more important than Dusty's, isn't it?'

'I suppose so,' Val admitted, and Rod tightened his grip upon her.

'Before we go any further, Val, let's get one thing straight,' he said quietly. 'Just what are you fighting *for*? Is it to get yourself revenged on Carson for him back-heeling you; is it to get Dusty out of a tight corner; or is it to use me to rescue Dusty so that you can find out about that gold mine from him no matter what lengths you have to go to?'

'What made you — think of the last bit?' Val's voice was half ashamed.

'Just the way you acted this morning. Hard-bitten — trying to be the little tough gal. I can imagine you wanting to know where gold is, but at the expense of your natural decency it isn't worth it, Val. If I thought that was your only aim I'd walk out right now and let this whole rotten set-up look after itself.'

Val was silent for a moment, her head drooping.

'I've been several kinds of a fool,' she whispered at last. 'I *did* send for you at first so that I could perhaps get you to rescue Dusty — then I thought I could get some information out of him . . . But that doesn't go any more, Rod. You can read me too clearly. Just try and find him and — and leave it at that. If he wants to be generous, OK. If not . . . Well, there it is.'

'That's more like the gal I first met,' Rod said, and with a sudden impulse he stooped and kissed her. Before she had recovered from her surprise he had swung her up to the saddle of his borrowed horse, and a moment afterwards had sprung up behind her . . .

4

Hell's Acres was more or less deserted when Rod, Bill, and the girl rode in. At this hour of mid-evening most of the folks were either in their own ranches or bunkhouses or else in The Last Frontier. At the moment it was the only place which cast forth a blaze of light into the street, the din of its activity floating out into the still night air.

Rod drew rein and studied the saloon closely, then he nodded to an upper window.

'That be his office, Val?' he enquired.

'Uh-huh,' she acknowledged. 'The office has two windows — one looking over the back veranda, and the other at the side. That's the side one.'

'Good enough. I reckon Bill and I can get in there. We don't want to give Carson the vaguest hint that we're coming. In the meantime we've got you to settle.'

This did not take long. Ma Gunthorpe, who had no regard for the gun-handy Carson anyway, took Val under her wing immediately when the circumstances were explained to her — and with double rent to cover whatever was needed in the way of extras until the girl recovered the old girl was quite satisfied.

'I'll be back later to see how you're making out, Val,' were Rod's closing words to her; then with a grim face he left the rooming house with Bill Tandrill beside him, walking the horses behind them, together with the mare. They fastened them to the tie-rail of the general stores next to the saloon — the stores being closed — and then exchanged looks.

'I'd feel a darned sight happier if I had my own hardware,' Bill complained. 'When it comes to the rough stuff I haven't much faith in these cheap guns we bought.'

'This won't be a matter of guns,' Rod told him quietly. 'I'm going to hand it back to Carson the way he gave it Val — with a horsewhip. Let's go! I reckon we've some climbing to do.'

To shin up the front of the veranda was only a moment's work for their agile limbs; then they crept together to the highest point of the sloping roof and worked their way along until they were directly over the lighted rectangle of the side window of the office.

'Apart from giving this guy Carson something to remember,' Rod said, 'I mean to get the information I want about Dusty Morgan at the same time. This business is draggin' on too long.'

He looked below him at the lighted window and then said:

'I'm taking a straight dive down and through. I should be able to make it. We don't stand a chance unless we get Carson on the hop. Follow me as best you can.'

Bill said nothing. He lay crouched and watching as Rod tensed himself; then he lowered himself until he was hanging by his hands. Swinging forward he kicked the glass out of the window with his heavy boots and then let himself drop in at an angle. He crashed stumblingly into Carson's office, a split second behind the glass shards and whipped out his gun simultaneously.

'Hold it, Carson!' he snapped, when the saloon owner's hand whipped down to his gun as he sat at his desk. Rod reflected swiftly the normal racket from the saloon should mask any sounds, so as not to alert Carson's men below, but as a precaution he went across to the door and threw the bolt over. A pair of feet swung into view across the broken window and in another moment Bill's tubby form came thumping inwards.

'Okay,' Rod snapped. 'Bill, take his hardware — and at the same time take ours. There it is on top of the safe. Might as well have what belongs to us.'

Carson sat watching narrowly and saying nothing. His hard lips tightened as his guns were taken from him.

'On your feet,' Rod ordered. 'An' keep your hands up!'

Carson obeyed. 'What's the idea?' he demanded. 'If yore aimin' to shoot me,

101

get on with it. I don't haveta stand up to be shot, do I?'

'I don't aim to shoot you, Carson.'

'How'd you get away from that tree?' he asked. 'It's got me puzzled.'

'Yeah? That's just too bad. Right now I don't aim to satisfy your curiosity. My concern is Val Kent and the things you did to her . . . Nice work for a guy who says he doesn't beat up women.'

Carson's expression changed. For a moment he even looked scared, then his normal truculence came back.

'Val Kent deserved all she got for the way she double-crossed me. Whatever you aim to do to me now doesn't matter much. It won't make her hurts any the easier!'

Rod smiled — a slow, murderous smile that made Carson stare at him fixedly. Deliberately, Rod put his gun back in the holster and then took down the horsewhip from the door.

'I don't know how many lashes you gave Val, Carson,' he said, 'but I daresay a dozen for you will about even things up. When I get through with you you won't be in a fit condition to speak, never mind beat anybody up. So before you're reduced to that state you're going to tell me something — Where Dusty Morgan is. Then just to back it up you'll take me to him. All right, start talking!'

With the snap of a pistol shot the long tail of the whip exploded violently before Carson's face. He jolted backwards, startled but unhurt, and came up hard against the big filing cabinet in the corner.

'A horsewhip can talk when you know how to handle it,' Rod explained, with still the same frozen smile. 'Bill here'll tell you I'm quite an expert.'

'He sure is,' Bill confirmed. 'He c'n knock the ash off a critter's cigar at five yards — '

The lash snapped again and this time the vicious end curled with fiendish force and sliced Carson mercilessly across the face. With a gasp of pain he flung his hand to his cheek.

'Well?' Rod asked, folding the lash back on itself dexterously. 'How do I get to Dusty Morgan?'

'Y'can cut me to pieces afore I'll tell you!' Carson snarled; then with a desperate look about him he charged suddenly for the big roll top, evidently intending to seek shelter behind it.

But he was not quick enough. The lash bit round his ankles and flung him from his feet. Before he could struggle up or scramble into hiding hell itself exploded across him — over his back, his thighs, his neck, and twice across his face as he twisted his head round desperately. Half blinded, wiping blood from his face with the back of his hand, he pressed himself flat on the floor as the murderous lash still belaboured him.

'Hold it!' he choked at last. 'For God's sake, Gayland, hold it — !'

Rod paused, the lash lying like a thin snake a foot from Carson's slashed features.

'I'm holding it,' Rod told him, his

voice merciless. 'What do you want to say?'

'I'll — I'll take you to Dusty Morgan! Leave me be, can't you?'

'OK. I reckon the lashes approximate those you gave Val. If I find I underpaid you I can always come back — Get him on his feet, Bill!'

Bill did so without ceremony and the gasping man shouted out loud as Bill's rough hands battered against his cut flesh. His shirt was in ribbons, two vivid wheals across his face. Rocking, he clutched the desk for support.

'You never were a beauty,' Rod told him briefly; 'and you look a darned sight worse right now. Get through that window, Carson, and down to the street. Last time you went through there it was Val who was too beaten up to stand: now it's you. And if you expect any tender treatment, forget it. You're going to ride like hell, and if the sweat runs salt into those cuts of yours it'll be just too bad . . . Get moving!'

'I-I can't,' Carson panted. 'Can't you

see when a guy's all through? I'd never make it to the shack!'

Reeling, he fell into a chair and then stiffened again with a gasp as the hard wooden back struck against him.

'Mebbe he's right, Rod,' Bill said, with a quick glance. 'If he passes out on us he'll be a hindrance, not a help.'

Rod strode across and seized the saloon owner by the front of his shirt.

'Where is this shack of yours, Carson? I'll find it quick enough — and if you hand me a bum steer I'll be back and get you for sure. On you giving the right answer depends your one slim hope of staying healthy a bit longer . . . '

'It's — it's at the top of the north arroyo,' Carson muttered, too weakened to resist any longer. 'We got half way there before when I fixed you to that tree — Keep on going up the rise until you hit the arroyo beyond the woodland. You can't miss it.'

'I'd better not!' Rod said bitterly. 'OK, I'll take a look. And I'll take your hardware with me . . . '

Without a sound Maninza became detached from the dense shadows of the trees around Carson's mountain shack. Some distance away, hidden in an outcropping, her pinto was tethered and motionless, trained to be as immobile as his mistress when occasion demanded.

A .32 in each hand, Maninza, in her usual red shirt and black pants, glided to the nearest window and stood for a moment contemplating the dull grey square which denoted the curtain masking the oil light beyond.

There were no sounds of voices, and outside here where she stood only the wind through the vegetation made any noise at all. She raised her right-hand gun, then smashed it down hard on the window glass and simultaneously whipped back the curtain. Straight down the gun barrel she stared into the startled faces of Pete and his two comrades as they sat playing cards before an upturned tub. Further away, near one of the joists supporting the ceiling, Dusty Morgan half hung out of his chair, the ropes still securing him.

'A dame!' Pete gasped abruptly, his hand blurring down to his gun; then he thought better of it as Maninza fired and blew his hat from his head.

'I shouldn't if I were you,' she said softly, and in the dim light the three men watched fixedly as she slid through the window and came towards them, her guns levelled.

'It's — Maninza!' one of the men ejaculated, seeing her clearly now for the first time.

'Yeah,' Pete whispered. 'The Redskin dame.'

'I have been around here several times,' she said, looking from one to the other sharply. 'I've been waiting until you had this prospector so weakened that he'll speak without much trouble. That's why I'm here. Since, when he speaks, his information might pass to you that makes it necessary that I eliminate you three. What information I get is for me alone.'

'Got mighty big ideas uv yuhself, ain't you?' Pete sneered.

The girl's black eyes glinted at him. 'I know just how far I can go,' she retorted, 'and I mean to! I — '

'Like hell!' Pete interrupted, and dived for her legs, low down.

Instead of flinging her on her back, as he had intended, an intolerable fire burst through his skull and he went sailing down into an endless gulf of blackness. Maninza stood amongst the fumes of her gun for a second, Pete's dead body a foot away from her — then her guns were snatched from her and her arms pinned behind her by the two remaining men.

'Yuh got Pete, but yuh don't git us!' one of them panted. 'Quick, Al — git some rope from over there . . . '

Al dashed to obey, and in that second Maninza acted; she twisted her slim, wiry body with amazing ease, flinging up her head so that it struck the gunman violently under the chin. His hold on her arms dislodged — and that was enough for Maninza. With the speed and sureness of trained ju-jitsu she grasped the gunman's wrist, twisted violently, and sent him flying backwards into the corner.

He had hardly landed with a crash against the stove, half the senses smashed out of him, before the remaining gunman hurtled forward. Maninza was ready for him. She bowed her body at the identical second he reached her. He stumbled, meeting no resistance; then the back of his neck was drawn down with savage power and he turned a complete somersault. Helplessly he fell against the table, his gun jolted out of his hand.

Maninza swung and dived, whirling up her gun and firing just as the man by the stove was taking aim. His gun dropped from his fingers as red suddenly stained his white check shirt across the breast. Stupidly he stared, and then relaxed.

'Wait a minnit!' panted the remaining man, as the dishevelled Aztec girl swung on him. 'I ain't done nothin' t'yuh, Miss Maninza. I only figgered to — '

Maninza's gun exploded again. She stood watching, smiling bitterly amidst the fumes, as the final gunman winced and then tumbled over helplessly on his face. Satisfied, she picked up the guns from the floor, jabbed them in her belt, and then went over to Dusty Morgan. Throughout the mêlée, he had only stirred but slightly, too weak to make a move. Maninza seized him under the chin, jerking it up, and stared down into his drawn, bruised face.

'Can you talk?' she snapped.

'I — I reckon I could if — if I had some water,' Dusty whispered through cracked lips. 'I ain't tasted none fur hell knows how long.'

Maninza strode across to the water jar, filled a tin cup, then brought it across. Supporting the old man's head she let him drink steadily. It brought life back to him as far as his expression was concerned, but his limbs were utterly

111

dead with cramp from the constricting ropes.

'Guess that feels better,' he panted. 'Thank you kindly, miss.' He looked at her blearily. 'I reckon yore Maninza, that Indian kid, ain't yuh? Not as it matters — Thanks fur takin' care uv them dirty critters on th' floor too.'

'Don't start running away with the wrong impression, Dusty,' Maninza said, banging the empty cup down on the table emphatically. 'I'm not saving you from anything. The information you didn't give to them you're going to give to me. I'm not here for any other reason. You have the whereabouts of an Aztec mine, and it rightfully belongs to me. Where is it?'

Dusty grinned hopelessly. 'Straight outa the fryin' pan inter th' fire, huh? I ain't tellin' yuh — any more'n I'd told them — or Carson when he lammed inter me.'

'I have ways of persuasion which these lunkheads never thought of,' Maninza said, watching him steadily. 'I shan't hesitate to use them if need be. I've given you water so you can speak — but I'm not doing anything more for you.'

Dusty looked at her fixedly, then his tired face quivered in contempt.

'Just like th' rest uv 'em, ain't yuh?' he demanded bitterly. 'Even if yuh are a woman an' s'posed ter be less tough than a man — '

'I can be as hard as any man — and harder, especially where the whites are concerned! If you doubt it, look at these three gunhawks I've taken care of!'

Dusty said nothing. Maninza set her thin, cruel mouth.

'Very well, since that's the way it is. I don't propose to try and get the truth out of you here because we may be interrupted. Where you need to be is the forest, where I can have a few trees to help me persuade you. You'll talk, Dusty Morgan, before I've finished with you!'

With her left hand, keeping the gun steady in her right, she removed her hunting-knife and slashed through Dusty's ropes. His limbs completely numb, he slipped from the chair and lay there, his face contorted at the surge of pins and needles through his veins. Maninza stood looking down on him cynically, her gun ready.

'Drop that gun, Maninza!'

She swung round and fired simultaneously as the command barked from the broken window. Rod, covering her, never expected such a lightning movement and more by chance than good shooting his gun was blown out of his tingling fingers.

'Good evening, Mr Gayland,' Maninza said politely, her dark eyes watching him narrowly. 'Come right inside! And if you have your friend with you bring him too — And no tricks!'

Rod compressed his lips and then scrambled through the broken window into the room, Bill coming after him. On the floor, Dusty began to stir slowly, life coming back into his limbs.

'Fur land's sake,' he whispered, 'how

many blasted critters are there a-chasin'
me?'

'I came to get you free, old timer,'
Rod told him, with a brief glance, 'but I
guess the lady has the drop on me this
time.'

'Correct,' she agreed. 'And keep your
hands up, the pair of you.'

'This doesn't tie up with you savin'
us from hanging, miss,' Bill pointed
out.

'I saved you so that you could go
after Drew Carson — not try and upset
my plans to learn the whereabouts of a
gold mine from Dusty here.'

'I'm as determined as you are,
Maninza, to know about that mine,'
Rod snapped. 'But only if Dusty's
willing to speak in his own free time. I
don't aim to beat it outa him.'

'No? Well, I do! Supposing you did
happen to learn what you want to
know: what would you do with the
gold?'

'Notify the authorities and have them
distribute it in the legal way.'

Maninza laughed shortly. 'The authorities!' she scoffed. 'By what right do *they* dare to cheat me out of my heritage? And, frankly, I don't believe you, Mr Gayland. I can't believe you're so utterly honest that you'd hand over a vast fortune in gold to authorities who are laden down with wealth already! Wealth which is mostly stolen!' she went on fiercely. 'The authorities belong to the race who drove my ancestors from these plains and smashed up their peace and security! Whatever gold there is is mine, and the few other Aztecs who still survive in this region! I'm going to make Dusty Morgan speak if I kill him by inches!'

Rod said nothing. The merciless vindictiveness of the Redskin girl was something with which he could not argue. He gave Bill a glance and he shrugged his fleshy shoulders.

'Get in that room!' Maninza snapped, waving the gun to the adjoining bedroom. 'I'm not risking tying up you two men: I'd probably not get away with it. All I want is time to get away with

116

Dusty, here. After that you can do as you like. You're still useful alive as long as you've no love for Drew Carson.'

With the gun trained on them there was nothing Rod and Bill could do except obey. They backed into the room and the door was slammed and locked after them, and not before Maninza had taken their guns from them.

'The window!' Bill said quickly, looking at it in the starlight. 'We can get through there.'

'Waste of time, Bill. She's got the guns — and the advantage. If we try and get her we'll get lead instead! Let her get clear first then we'll track her as best we can . . .'

They moved to the window quickly and stood watching while in the dim light Maninza appeared outside, Dusty shambling before her at the point of her gun. He mounted one of the horses outside — Bill's — and Maninza kept beside him until she came to her pinto in the nearby outcropping. Then they both vanished from sight, the darkness enveloping them.

'OK,' Rod said quickly. 'Here we go — ' He paused with his elbow raised to smash it through the window glass. 'Say, wait a minute! Somebody coming! Better not give ourselves away too quickly.'

Speeding horsemen resolved out of the gloom and came to a stop outside the shack, apparently looking at Rod's solitary mount fastened to the tie-rail.

'It's Carson!' Bill muttered. 'An' some of his boys! You made a mistake in leaving him behind to do as he liked! Guess it doesn't pay t'be soft-hearted with a snake like that.'

'Uh-huh.' Rod was watching keenly. 'Let the boys come into the shack and we'll get out quick this way . . . '

But the plan did not work. Carson and one of the men entered the shack; the two others remaining on guard outside. Before Rod or Bill could think of a way out of the situation the door of the room was unlocked and, defenceless, the two were facing Carson's guns, his colleague standing by the table beyond.

'Well!' Carson sneered. 'Ain't this nice! The boyfriend and his fat-bellied sidekick all ready and waiting . . .Where's Dusty?' he broke off savagely.

Rod shrugged, watching the saloon owner narrowly.

'Maninza took him — God knows where. She means to make him talk.'

'Am I supposed to believe that?' Carson came forward a little, his gun ready, patches of plaster on his face hiding the whip lashes across it.

'Please yourself. It's true. Bill and I got here just as she was releasing Dusty to take him away.'

'Talk sense!' Carson roared. 'D'yuh expect me t'believe that a woman the size uv Maninza could kill three uv my boys and lock you two men in this room, *and* take Dusty away too? I ain't that crazy! More likely *you* shot the boys in here and then got the truth outa Morgan and let him go. You saw us comin' and locked yourselves in here. There weren't no key in the lock. I had t'use my spare one to get in.'

'You take a lot of convincing,' Rod said quietly. 'All this time Maninza's getting further away, and I think she will make Dusty talk. She doesn't behave like any woman we know, Carson. She's dynamite!'

'Shut up about Maninza and talk sense! I know she's tricky but she ain't the superwoman you'd have me think. I'll lay evens she's not been anywheres near here — Out with it! How much did yuh find out from Dusty afore he escaped on one of the horses outside — leaving one at the tie-rail?'

'You've had the facts, Carson,' Rod snapped. 'If you won't believe 'em I can't help it.'

The man in the room beyond, who had been listening to the conversation, came forward.

'Not much use wastin' time on this jigger, boss. He'll not speak no matter how hard you try. Best thing we c'n do is get on Dusty's trail while it's still fresh.'

Carson reflected briefly then nodded. 'OK. Mebbe yore right. Before we do it though we might as well do a bit of tidying up. I reckon dead bodies should be cremated — an' it'd save a lot of trouble if these two live ones went with 'em. Get these guys fastened up, Harry.'

Harry obeyed. In five minutes Rod and Bill were both fastened immovably back to back and were lying helplessly on the floor.

'OK,' Carson grinned, and delivered a kick into Rod's ribs. 'Mebbe what's coming to you, Gayland, 'll pay you back for the whipping y'gave me. When the flames start burnin' around you just think of Val Kent an' the things I mean t'do to her afore I'm finished!'

With that he strode out of the room and from their position on the floor Rod and Bill saw the oil lamp flung to the boards. It exploded instantly into flame, the fire sweeping quickly to the bone-dry tinders and destroying the curtains in clouds of sparks.

In the space of a few seconds the fire

had a complete hold on the shack's living room and spread beyond it to the door of the bedroom. Savagely the two men on the floor fought to break free of their ropes, but it was a hopeless proposition.

'Looks like Carson had all the aces up his sleeve,' Bill panted, breathing hard. 'We're not going to get outa this one, Rod!'

Rod had not given up struggling yet. He fought and strained and pulled, coughing as smoke surged into his lungs. Pausing in his efforts for a moment he watched in alarm as the nearby bed went up in a cloud of smoke and roaring flame. Fear began to get him as the flames twisted and writhed across the floor towards him.

'Rod! *Rod!*' came the scream of a girl's voice — and he could hardly hear it above the crackling din of the fire.

He tried to twist around, realizing the cry had come from the smashed window — but movement was useless. Then suddenly there was the thump of a body dropping to the wooden floor and Val Kent became visible moving painfully from the maltreatment she had received earlier from Carson.

She stooped and pulled savagely at the knots on the ropes which bound the two men. By the time she had tugged the knots free the flames were no more than a yard away. Without a word Rod got on his feet, then holding the girl's arm he stumbled to the window with Bill bringing up in the rear. Frantically they scrambled through it and dropped into the cool night air.

'Whew!' Rod whistled, when they had released his own and the girl's horse from the tie rack. 'That was mighty close! How on earth did you manage it, Val?'

She laughed rather shakily, staring at the blaze cascading into the night.

'I happened to see Carson and his boys setting off from town. I was in my room at the time, looking out of the window, just at the end of bandaging myself up. I guessed he wouldn't be setting off like that without good reason so I thought I'd better follow. I kept track part of the way, then lost them. It was fire from this shack that finally led me to you — and thank heaven it did.'

'That we're mighty grateful goes without saying,' Rod said, 'and especially since you're not in any condition to do much riding . . . '

'I'm all right,' Val interrupted. 'Ma Gunthorpe patched me up fine — but if she finds me gone, and one of her best horses too, she'll probably wonder what's going on.'

'If you ask me,' Bill said, watching the flames, 'we'll be lucky if we're not caught in a forest fire the way things're going!'

Rod and Val did not answer. Recovering their breath they stood watching the holocaust — but Bill's guess was wrong. The rocky area around the shack absorbed most of the sparks and flames and presently the blaze began to die down.

'Well, that's one relief, anyway,' Bill

said finally. 'What happens now?'

'We get Val back to town,' Rod decided, but to his surprise the girl protested.

'That's just what I don't want, Rod! I was on pins all the time you were absent, wondering what had happened to you. I just can't stand the suspense. I'd sooner be with you and see what's going on, even if I do ache all over.'

'Well, mebbe you'd be safer with us at that,' Rod admitted. 'OK, you can ride that horse you came on and Bill and I will ride double-saddle on the remaining one. Right now we've one job — and one only — to finish.'

As the girl looked at him questioningly in the diminishing glare of the fire he told her of all that had happened.

'So that means we've got to find Dusty somehow and save him from both Maninza and, if need be, Carson,' Rod explained. 'I guess we've no guns but we'll have to risk it.'

'I've this thirty-two,' Val said, taking it from her belt. 'All I had time to get before chasing after Carson.'

Rod took it. 'It'll help . . . OK, let's see if we can pick up the signs of the way Maninza and Dusty went.'

5

Steadily, directed by Maninza's orders as she rode immediately behind him, Dusty Morgan drove his horse through the dark woodlands which sprawled throughout the foothills of Paradise Mountains. Though he rode with a drooping head and shoulders, conveying the impression of utter listlessness, he was a good deal more alert than Maninza realized. In spite of the ordeal he had undergone, Dusty Morgan was of whipcord physique, and the fresh night wind and the drink he had been given had combined to revive him considerably. He kept his wits about him as he rode, waiting for the chance of a break-away.

'How far do yuh reckon t'take me?' he asked after a while, without turning his head.

'Far enough away from that shack for you not to be interfered with — or me either . . . ' Maninza stopped in mid-sentence as, in glancing behind her, she noticed a flaring of sparks and a quivering red glow in the distance. It held her attention for a moment as she realized it must be the shack itself further down the slope beyond the woodland —

Then suddenly her wrist was seized and wrenched violently. Her gun twisted out of her hand and a shove knocked her from the saddle. She landed with a thump in a sitting position to find Dusty standing over her, hardly visible in the dim light.

'Reckon I don't often knock a lady about,' he said drily, 'but this time I figger it's justified. I wasn't so dopey as yuh figgered, Maninza.'

'No . . . apparently not!' She got on her feet slowly watching the glint from Dusty's steadily-aimed gun — her own.

'I reckon I've better things t'do than trail along just where yuh want me to go,' Dusty added, 'so I'll be on mv way. Just in case yuh get ideas I'll take yore cayuse with me.'

He grasped its reins and, walking backwards so he could keep the girl covered, returned to his own horse. Mounting swiftly, he dug in the spurs and set the animal speeding forward amidst the trees, Maninza's pinto cantering along in the rear as the reins pulled on him.

Her fists clenched, Maninza watched the old prospector disappearing. For a moment or two she stood deciding what to do next — whether to return to her ranch or try and follow the old man. Finally she decided on the latter course. Though he had a big start on her, and could maintain it on a horse, there must be a point where he would finally rest, and that might be her chance. With her hereditary gifts of tracking she was pretty sure that she could still remain on his trail.

She began moving, examining the trees and the ground as she went. Here and there she had to strike a match to more closely examine a hoof-print, an overturned stone, or some other slight but telling evidence of Dusty's passage upwards into the higher reaches of the hills. It occurred to her that he would probably seek one of the mountain caves wherein to sleep. If so she would overtake him before the night was out.

Half an hour later, however, the sounds of horses' hoofs crashing through the undergrowth brought her sharply to attention. She made an effort to dodge into concealment, but Drew Carson had seen her, even though he did not instantly identify her sex.

'Take it easy!' he commanded, firing a single shot skywards as a warning. 'Stand right where you are.'

With his three cohorts beside him he presently came over to where Maninza stood waiting, her hands slightly raised, dark fury in her eyes.

'Well, if this ain't luck!' Carson ejaculated, cuffing up his hat. 'Maninza! Rod Gayland and this Indian dame all in one night: that's mighty fortunate.'

'Looks like Gayland may have bin

speaking th' truth, boss, when he said this dame was mixed up in things,' one of the men remarked.

'Yeah,' Carson agreed, thinking. 'Could be — ' He swung on the girl. 'Where's old Dusty Morgan?' he demanded. 'How much did you get to know from him?'

Maninza remained silent. Carson gave a chuckle.

'Okay, gal, if that's how you feel about it. I reckon we might as well see what you can tell us before we follow Dusty's trail any further. I sure reckon you wouldn't have let him get away if you hadn't gotten all the information you needed outa him. I guess we can camp right here for the moment,' Carson added, looking about the clearing. 'Good enough spot — an' quiet. And we'll make you talk, Maninza, before we're through. OK, boys, tie her up for the moment while I think out what t'do with her.'

Before long all four men were sprawled in the soft undergrowth, their horses tethered to the trees. Maninza, her hands tightly bound behind her, sat with her back to the bole of a tree, her lips tight and her eyes gleaming.

'Everything's workin' out very nicely, I guess,' Carson murmured to his cohorts. 'Saves us trackin' Dusty half across the earth now we've got her. She must know all about the mine or that old jigger would never have gotten away from her — But she's tough stuff to break down. Not like an ordinary woman who'd yell if she even got her face smacked.'

'She's flesh an' blood, even if she is Aztec,' one of the men growled. 'I guess even she'd speak if I slowly broke her arm fur her.'

'Try it,' Carson grinned, and sat back to watch the proceedings in the dawning moonlight.

The puncher went across to the girl, unfastened her wrists, and took one of her arms in his powerful fingers — The next thing he knew he had been flung over the girl's head and landed with his face in the undergrowth, his mouth full of soil.

Carson guffawed, his gun playing on the girl as she hesitated at making further moves.

'Guess yore not going to get far that way, Hank,' Carson said drily. 'The gal knows all the tricks. Mebbe I've got it, though. You two follow out my instructions while I keep her covered,' he added, to the men either side of him.

They obeyed, following out his instructions to the letter. When they had finished Maninza was standing under a tree branch, her hands securely tied behind her again and a cord round her neck knotted to the branch. To save herself being throttled she had to stand on tip-toe. The slightest relaxation made the cord slip-knot about her throat draw tight.

Carson grinned sadistically as he looked at her.

'Think that one over, sweetheart,' he said, settling down near her and lighting a cigarette. 'When your tootsies get tired and you feel like talking about the mine let me know. Otherwise you stop right where you are!'

Not a word escaped the stoic Indian girl. She stood on tip-toe the cord slack about her neck, watching the four men as they sprawled talking among themselves. At first she had no difficulty in maintaining her attitude, but gradually her feet began to ache and pain crept up her calves. She relaxed very slightly — and the slip-knot glided on her neck. Instantly she drew up sharp again, setting her teeth against the growing torment in her legs.

'She'll talk,' Carson murmured confidently, with a glance at her. 'That's an old Chinese stunt I've worked on her an' it's a beaut. I've read up on such things. Never know when you want 'em in this part of the world . . . '

He yawned and stretched himself, then put his hands behind his head and lay watching the Aztec girl's desperate efforts to keep on her toes. His three cohorts watched too, grinning among themselves, so intent on their villainy they did not hear or see the silent gliding of three figures towards them out of the undergrowth.

'Easy!' Rod Gayland breathed, gripping the arms of Bill and Val worming along beside him. 'They're down here . . . Carson and the boys. In this clearing. I didn't imagine it when I heard voices.'

Bill glanced uneasily behind him. 'Hope those blasted horses of ours don't start whinnying. If they do we don't stand a chance.'

'Get back to them, Val,' Rod whispered. 'I've only got this thirty-two to fight with if it comes to gunplay and I don't want anything giving us away.'

'OK,' Val murmured, and began to retreat.

Silent, worming over the undergrowth, Rod and Bill moved forward again until they could see the clearing without interference. The moonlight was sufficiently powerful now for the figure of Maninza to be visible too.

'She's there too!' Bill whispered in astonishment. 'What have they done to her? Hanged her — No, she moved,' he added. 'I don't get it.'

'I think I do, though,' Rod breathed. 'The dirty no-account swines are torturing her — ' His hand withdrew the .32 from his belt and he handed it to Bill. 'Here, take this. I'm going to use my fists to try and gain the surprise advantage. If you have to fire to keep me from being shot do it. Here I go . . . '

He stood up, measured his distance, then with a flying leap hurtled down from his higher elevation. As he fell he threw both his arms wide so that as he landed each arm encircled the neck of Carson and the man nearest him. With fiendish force Rod slammed the heads of the two men together, half stunning them with the impact.

One of the other men whipped out his gun, fired, and missed. The fourth man found himself hit by the massive figure of Bill Tandrill and a terrific haymaker to the jaw snapped back his head as though it were on a hinge.

Carson, dazed, overtaken by surprise, grabbed at his gun, but it did not avail him anything. Rod seized him by the front of his shirt, dragged him up, and then punched him in the face with every vestige of his iron strength. Carson staggered backwards on his heels and crashed on his back. But he was not knocked out by a long way. Again he dived his hand for his gun but Rod's heavy boot came down on his forearm and numbed it with a vicious kick.

Then Carson's guns were gone. Holding them, Rod dashed over to the Indian girl and with his knife slashed through the rope which held her neck. She relaxed on to the soles of her feet and breathed hard.

'Repayment for you saving my pardner and me,' Rod told her swiftly. 'No more, no less — ' He cut the ropes that bound her hands. 'I'll talk to you in a minute.'

He swung back to the attack, his guns ready — but in the interval Carson had got on his feet. At the identical moment of Rod turning, the saloon owner landed a right-hander which spun Rod in a half circle and dropped him to his knees. Another brutal blow across the back of the neck half paralyzed him for a moment — and the guns he had snatched had gone.

'On your feet!' Carson snarled, digging the gun into Rod's ribs as he tried to get his senses straightened out. 'Hurry it up, damn you!'

Slowly Rod obeyed, and gradually realized how completely he had lost the advantage. The remaining men — save the one whom Bill had utterly knocked out — were on their feet too, their guns at the ready. Maninza stood nearby motionless, and Bill was perhaps a yard from her, dishevelled and his hands raised.

Rod looked about him anxiously, wondering how much of the battle Val had seen and what she would do now. Certainly she would commit suicide if she walked into a set-up like this. Her

138

best move would be to hit leather for Hell's Acres as fast as she could and fetch the sheriff and posse to clear up the mess —

In actuality Val had no idea what had occurred. She had such faith in Rod she had assumed he would be the master of the situation and given her attention to something else. At the moment she was riding swiftly towards a distant moonlit rimrock whereupon, only a short while before — when she had returned to keep the horses quiet — she had seen a solitary rider moving slowly. That it was Dusty Morgan she had not the least doubt, evidently on his way to the mountain cleft which finally opened out on to the plain beyond the range.

For the moment Val was only thinking of one thing — the sole thing which had been motivating her from the very start — Gold. To which Dusty Morgan had the answer. If she could only catch up with him —

She ignored her own aches and pains, enhanced by the jolting she got in the saddle, and rode like the wind across the comparatively flat terrain between herself and the rimrock.

After a while the going became tougher as she forced the horse up an acclivity, but all the time the rimrock came nearer . . . Dusty Morgan — for Val had been right in her guess — presently heard her coming, the high walls of the cleft in which he was riding catching the hoofbeats of Val's speeding horse somewhere in the rear. Dusty drew to a halt and looked behind him.

All he could see at the moment were the peaks climbing into the bright moonlit sky — then unexpectedly he caught sight of the pursuing rider, a lone figure high up on the rocks and coming in his direction, her hair streaming in the wind.

'Fur land's sakes — Maninza!' he whispered. 'That sneakin' Indian dame musta gotten herself a hoss some place . . . '

He could be forgiven his mistake in the uncertain light — and the thought of meeting up again with the remorse-less Aztec girl was enough to set him going forward once more at top speed. So as not to be too encumbered in his flight he released the reins of the Indian girl's pinto which he was trailing along beside him.

Val, swinging her horse into the cleft, saw the sudden spurt which Dusty had put on and goaded her sweating, snorting mount to even greater efforts. In a cloud of dust, stumbling here and there over loose stones, the animal hurtled onwards. In the deep shadows ahead Dusty presently vanished, to reappear urging his horse along a difficult trail skirting the mountain face.

Val drew rein and watched, horrified. Knowing the district as well as she did she knew too the frightful risk Dusty was taking. Probably he was aware of it, since he knew the terrain as intimately as she did.

'Dusty, come back here!' she yelled, cupping her hands. 'It's me — Val!'

Dusty heard the shouting, but not

the words, and looked back over his shoulder. In that instant he momentarily lost control over his almost stampeded horse and the animal slipped on the perilous path, made a desperate effort to save itself, then went lunging out into space.

Frozen in her saddle Val watched the scene against the moonlight, of man and rider hurtling downwards into the canyon skirting the mountain trail. She covered her eyes for a moment. When she looked again horse and rider had gone and there was the silence of the night.

'He — he wouldn't run from me like that,' Val whispered, her eyes a little moist as she gazed into the gloom of the canyon ahead. 'He must have mistaken me for somebody else — Maybe Maninza.'

She debated for a while whether or not to explore the canyon ahead and see if she could find the body; then realizing how long and difficult a task it would be by moonlight — and probably useless anyway — she turned back on her tracks and headed towards the spot where she had left Rod and Bill about to deal with Carson and his boys.

The remaining horse was still where she had left it, tied to the tree, but of Rod or Bill there was no sign. Puzzled, not a little alarmed, she dismounted and crept forward through the undergrowth to the spot where she had left Rod and Bill preparing for action.

The sight of the clearing below froze her into immobility.

Rod and Bill were unharmed, as yet, but obviously bound. They were seated between Carson and his three cohorts whilst under a nearby tree branch Maninza was again standing on tip-toe with a rope about her neck.

Carson spoke, and his words carried clearly since the Indian girl was some distance away.

'If we sit here all night, sweetheart, it makes no odds. Now we've got this guy Gayland and his sidekick with us we can be sure of gettin' no interference. If you don't talk quick mebbe I'll add a little seasoning — like splinters jammed down your fingernails f'instance.'

Val winced as she crouched listening. She debated swiftly what she ought to do, then hesitated as Carson got to his feet and went over to where the Indian girl was struggling to keep the rope from tightening about her throat.

'Feel like talkin'?' he asked pleasantly. 'I don't aim to waste all night, y'know!'

All he received was the cold gleam of her dark eyes in the moonlight. He grinned and took a box of matches from his pocket. Still grinning he removed one and began to shave it with his knife to a needle-thin splinter.

'You've one last chance to talk, Maninza, before I really go to work on you!' he grated at her, his grin vanishing.

Val looked about her desperately. Whatever risk it might entail she was prepared to hurl a stone at Carson — anything to stop his sadism.

'All right,' Carson said, and taking the Indian girl's right hand as it lay tied to her left behind her back he forced her fingers upwards. As the splinter touched her index fingernail she gave a hoarse gasp.

'Wait!' she choked. 'I'll — I'll tell you!'

'Go on talking,' Carson ordered deliberately, the point of the splinter pricking the edge of her nail.

'Cut me free and I'll take you straight to the mine. You win, Carson. I can't stand any more of this.'

Carson hesitated and then threw the splinter away. Keeping the gun in his right hand as a precaution he eased his knife into his left and slashed through the girl's ropes. She relaxed and stood breathing hard, casting off the deadly noose from about her throat.

'The mine's about a mile from here,' she said, nodding vaguely westwards, 'I can take you straight to it.'

Rod and Bill looked at one another in puzzlement, then got on their feet as they were nudged by the gunmen on either side of them. Above, securely

145

hidden, Val watched the proceedings intently.

'OK, we'll go,' Carson said. 'If you're pulling some game, Maninza, so much the worse for you.'

'Just a minnit, boss,' one of the men protested. 'What happens to these two jiggers? We don't want them to know where the mine is too, do we?'

'They won't,' Carson said grimly. 'They'll come with us because I'm not takin' the risk of leaving them behind: they might get free like they did last time. Once we've found the mine we'll dispose of 'em . . . Now let's go. We've wasted quite enough time already.'

The men gathered the horses together and presently, led by Maninza, the entire party began to get on the move from the clearing. Val watched them until they were some distance away, then she returned for the two horses and, leading them behind her, she followed the trail the party made and kept at a safe distance.

Without uttering a word Maninza kept progressing, breaking clear of the

146

woodland at length and coming out into the rocky, empty stretches of the true foothills. Here there was nothing but jagged grey tableland and the pallid light of the moon.

'I'll gamble everything I've got she doesn't know where the mine is,' Bill muttered, as he walked along beside Rod — both of them with their wrists firmly bound behind them. 'And if she's leading Carson up the garden path she's taking one hell of a risk.'

Evidently Carson was thinking pretty much the same thing for he presently called a halt and jammed his gun in Maninza's slim back.

'Where th' heck are you taking us?' he demanded. 'I know this territory pretty well an' I'll swear there's no mine round here. I'd have found it long ago if there had ha' been.'

'It's quarter of a mile ahead of us, in a gully,' Maninza replied coldly. 'Up to you whether you want to go to it, or not.'

'Well — OK,' Carson muttered

— and the journey continued.

Until, much to the surprise of Carson, and Rod and Bill too for that matter, they found upon descending a steep slope that was blocked at one end by a massive copper door, obviously a relic of an old-time civilization.

'Genuine Aztec,' Carson breathed, peering at the door intently. 'The Aztecs usta guard many of their mines with copper doors. I don't know how I ever came to miss this one.'

'You missed it because it's hidden under a rock ledge,' the Indian girl told him. 'You can't see it from above; and from the level, in daylight, this gully looks like a dead end. I'm possibly the only one who can open this door, too.'

'Then how come Dusty Morgan got inside and took out a gold nugget?' Carson snapped, suspicious.

It seemed to Rod and Bill that the girl hesitated for a fraction of a second, but in his eagerness Carson apparently did not notice it.

'He found another way in — by the underground. He told me about it . . . under pressure, of course. We could go in that way ourselves but this is easier. I know the combination to this door.'

'Just a moment — ' Carson caught the girl's arm roughly. '*How* d'you know the combination? I'll gamble Dusty didn't tell you that much — so what's the explanation?'

'All the doors of the mines owned by the Aztecs have the same combination. As an Aztec I know what that combination is. Now do you want the door opened, or don't you?'

'OK,' Carson growled, releasing her. 'Hurry it up!'

Maninza stepped into the gloom in front of the door and began to fiddle with the mighty ornamental handle.

'Something phony here,' Rod muttered. 'I don't credit that Maninza hasn't known of this mine for long enough. I get the impression she's no information at all and this is nothin' but elaborate stalling — but where it gets her I don't know. Or us either.'

He said no more for at this moment the door opened with a creaking of age-old hinges. Warm air gushed out of the darkness — air which smelled of the tomb.

'This way,' Maninza murmured, and crept into the darkness with Carson, Rod, Bill, and the remaining men coming up behind.

'How far in?' Carson demanded after a moment or two.

There was no answer. Carson swore and came to a stop, swinging round to look at the moonlit rectangle where the door lay open. He was just in time to see a slender figure silhouetted against the grey glow; then the door swung inwards ponderously and locked itself.

'Hey!' Carson yelled savagely. 'Blast you! Hey — you — '

He staggered in the pitchy darkness and beat savagely on the door's metalwork.

'I guess you needn't waste your time, Carson,' Rod said grimly. 'She's got the drop on us beautifully and you walked right into it and brought us with you. We're sealed in here, an' here we'll stop unless a miracle happens.'

'Like hell we will!' the saloon owner retorted and after a moment he became visible holding a match high above his head. The wavering glimmer made him look disembodied against the all-surrounding black.

'That dame musta known of this place for years,' one of the men snapped. 'She led us into it then doubled back. If there's a way outa this hole nobody'll be more surprised'n me!'

Rod did not say anything. He gave Bill a glance and then the sputtering match went out . . .

Meanwhile Maninza was moving silently away from the massive door and smiling to herself. She imagined she was quite alone, until the sudden whinnying of a horse from somewhere on the ledge above the gully made her glance up quickly. She was just in time to see a head withdrawn.

Her heart racing with alarm — chiefly because she was unarmed — Val hurried over to where she had tethered the horses after following the party this far; but long before she could unfasten the reins and make a getaway the figure of Maninza appeared a little distance away and came forward with a levelled gun.

Val relaxed and waited, her face set. Presently the Indian girl had come right up to her, the moonlight casting on her hard, inscrutable face.

'So it's you, Miss Kent,' she murmured. 'It isn't any great surprise, either. Good job the horse gave you away — though I hardly think you'd be able to open that mine door without the combination. Still, you could have gone for help and explosives, I suppose.'

'Just what are you driving at, Maninza?' Val demanded, feeling that perhaps nothing would be lost if she became bold. 'I saw you drive Carson and his men into that mine — and that I can understand. Far as I'm concerned they can rot there. But why do it to Rod Gayland and his friend? What have they ever done to you?'

'They are white,' Maninza answered simply, as though that explained everything.

'That doesn't mean that you — '

'Listen to me!' Maninza interrupted harshly. 'Carson and his men tortured me. They'd have killed me if necessary. So I told them I'd take them to a gold mine. I have done so; but the gold in it was taken out years ago. Now they're inside a mine — of which there are hundreds scattered about this state — from which there is no escape. Rod Gayland and his friend are there too because I had no time to discriminate. There they'll stop. Not so long ago Gayland was in danger of death — and I saved him. Tonight he tried to save me. That evened the score. I owe him nothing. If he smothers in that mine with Carson that doesn't concern me . . . In fact the only thing concerning me now is . . . you.'

'I — I haven't done anything!' Val said, hesitantly.

'So far, no — but you'd like to. You'd like to race back to town and get help, and that is the one thing I don't intend to allow. I've got to kill you, Miss Kent, to protect my own interests.'

Val could think of nothing to say. She watched fascinatedly as the Aztec girl's gun glinted in the moonlight and aimed straight at her heart . . .

★ ★ ★

'The sooner you call an armistice between us, Carson, the better,' Rod Gayland said from the darkness of the mine. 'Cut these ropes from Bill an' me and we'll help look for a way out. We can't do a thing like this.'

'Yeah?' Carson's voice was bitter. 'Soon as I cut you loose you'll be up to your tricks, an' I'm not taking the chance.'

Rod lost his temper. 'Don't be such a damned fool, man! What chance have

Bill and I of gettin' outa here even we did set about you and your boys? And anyways, how could we when you've got all the hardware? This isn't a personal feud any more, Carson; it's trouble for all of us unless we can get out.'

'Okay,' Carson grunted, and struck another match. 'Untie 'em, Al.'

The ropes were unfastened and Rod and Bill stood for a moment massaging their wrists. Carson lighted another match from the first one.

'Well?' he demanded, peering. 'Now you're free what bright ideas have you got for getting outa here?'

'To start with,' Rod said, 'there's a draught. You can't feel it so much now, but I noticed it when the mine door was first opened.'

'So what?'

'Use your brains, Carson,' Rod snapped. 'You never ever get a draught without two open ends. Somewhere there's another opening where air gets through, and it's up to us to find it.

Best thing we can do is feel our way in the dark and conserve matches. I've a few I can use when yours run out.' Their personal enmity forgotten in their common plight all the men linked hands and began to move forward slowly, feeling their way along the floor with the toes of their boots as they progressed. It was the only way they could be sure that they would not suddenly plunge into a cleft and instant death.

As they went they realized the true extent of the space in which they were entombed. It was no small area. Even their voices echoed, and Rod calculated that it took them at least fifteen minutes before they finally hit up against a wall. Some groping and match-striking revealed to them that a tunnel mouth gaped only a few yards away. They felt their way towards it and came immediately into a noticeable draught.

'Looks like you were right, Gayland,' Carson admitted grudgingly. 'Opening somewheres to account for this. Better see what we can find.'

Still with linked hands they went forward into the tunnel's blackness. Now and again Carson struck a match and looked about him on to dusty, age-old walls. After a while he gave a growl of disgust.

'Not a blasted sign of gold anywheres! Maninza sure double-crossed us all right!'

'If you'd have had the brains of a gnat you'd have seen that,' Rod told him. 'All she did was lead us into an abandoned mine from the Aztec period. Even if she ever got information about the real bonanza from Dusty Morgan — which I doubt — you don't suppose she would hand it on to you, do you?'

'I reckon she would if I persuaded her long enough.'

'Don't try conclusions with an Aztec woman again, Carson, if you ever get out of this,' Rod advised him. 'She can beat you every time . . . '

Carson did not say any more. He had quite enough worrying him at the moment.

When presently he spoke again he stopped in mid-sentence, surprised at the echo from his voice.

'Looks like we've come to another cavern,' he said — and another precious match flared up.

The extent of this new cavern was so huge that the match was useless.

'We'd best break up and search around,' Rod advised. 'The draught's coming from some place around here and one of us might find it.'

'Yeah, an' if it's you I can see you telling me about it,' Carson sneered.

'As long as you've a nose on your face you can find it if I can,' Rod retorted. 'Anyways I'm going to take a look.'

He set off into the dark with Bill beside him. For a long time afterwards matches flared at intervals from different areas of the great cave, until Rod at least had formed a fair mental picture of the surroundings. They were in a natural cavern, its roof supported by mighty rock pillars. Around the walls were deep ledges, hewn out by volcanic activity in some forgotten era of time.

And there was a way out. Rod was the first to find it.

6

With Bill Tandrill by his side Rod stood looking at a narrow opening, the match spluttering in his fingers as he did so. In the brief time both men had to study the gap they could see it was extremely narrow — and dangerous. It meant squirming through a three-foot slit into whatever lay beyond, and too much struggling in the process might easily dislodge the single thin needle of rock which supported a load of countless tons and made the gap possible.

How it had come into being was a mystery. It might even be a blowhole created by explosions in the past when the mine had been workable. Right now it was a tiny egress to possible freedom, a warm wind blowing strongly through it.

'You mugs found something?'

Rod turned sharply at the crunching

of heavy feet on the stony floor. Drew Carson struck a match and with his men behind him stood peering at the opening.

'Looks like it might be worth gettin' through,' he commented: then as if to prevent any further argument he took out his gun and pointed it at Rod. 'We're back where we started, Gayland,' he said. 'If you try anything I'll get you for sure.'

'Not very likely when I've no gun, is it?' Rod asked sourly. 'And I'm telling you something — If you look at that hole closely you'll see you don't stand a cat in hell's chance of getting through it. You're too damned big.'

'An' I suppose yore not?' Carson asked, grinning. 'And what about this fat bag of blubber with you?'

'Neither he nor I nor you can get through there,' Rod stated. 'Best let that thin sidekick of yours try it . . . ' and he nodded to the tall, slim being whom Carson called Al.

'Let him get through while we stop

here?' Carson demanded. 'Like hell!'

'He can go and get help,' Rod pointed out. 'If he can find his way to the outside the only thing he's got to do is get some explosives from town, come back, and blow the door to Hades. There isn't any other way.'

'There'd better be,' Carson said grimly. 'I wouldn't trust any of these coyotes out of my sight for five minutes. With me in here and one of 'em outside we'd be left to starve and then the one who was free would come back, weeks later, and look for whatever gold there might be lying around.'

'There isn't any,' Bill Tandrill said. 'And you damned well know it! Stop stalling, Carson, and let Al go. He's the only one who can make it.'

Al struck one of his own matches and stepped forward to the gap, but Carson caught his shoulder and swung him round.

'Wait a minute, you! Where do you think yore going?'

'But I thought I had to.'

'I'll give the orders here, see? Get back! If anybody's going through that hole, I am.'

'Do that,' Rod warned, 'and you're liable to kill yourself and finish it for all of us.'

'I'll take durned good care I don't kill myself. As for leaving the lot of you in a spot, I should worry! None of you matter a damn to me, anyways. And I still figger there might be gold in this dump somewheres when I can come back and look for it in peace.'

Al clenched his fists, and so did his two companions. The match Carson was holding went out and he struck another one hastily. His revolver ready in case an effort was made to stop him he moved to the gap and began to ease himself through it backwards so he could keep his gun trained on the men eyeing him.

None of the men fired at him; they were too fascinated in watching him, and they also realized he could still fire back . . . and be unlikely to miss at such close quarters. When Carson's match expired Rod struck one himself and held the flame close so he could observe Carson's squirming movements. By this time he had got through the hole to his waist and the rock was pinning him gently but firmly on all sides.

'Who said I couldn't get through?' he sneered, his arms extended in front of him to narrow his width and his gun still in his hand. 'I'll durned soon — '

His sentence was cut short by the sudden explosion of Al's gun. Realizing the match Carson was holding had nearly expired, and that Carson was in a position which made firing difficult, the gunhawk seized his chance. He did not fire directly at his boss, but at the single pillar of rock supporting the load over the gap.

The bullet struck the base of the thin but immensely strong prop, chipping a V-shaped wedge out of it.

'You dirty — !' Carson yelled, and that was as far as he got. The match expired, his gun exploded futilely; then he screamed horribly out of the darkness as in his jolting movement to see how much damage Al had caused he shifted the rock pillar from its base.

Rod and Bill stood sweating in the blackness as Carson's dying scream broke into a choking gasp which became silence. The rumble of shifting rock died away. A match glowed again through the haze of dust.

'Hell's bells,' Al whispered. 'I reckon it sure got him!'

Rod and Bill looked at the motionless head and shoulders of Carson projecting from the debris, his hand dangling limply. Blood had frothed the rocks.

'Serve the dirty critter right,' Al added venomously. 'He figgered on leaving us to disaster; instead he got it himself.'

'Hardly instead,' Rod said, staring at the gunman in the match-light. 'As long as that hole remained, even if Carson had gotten through, we stood a chance. Now we don't stand any.'

'What's ter stop us heaving the rocks outa the way?' one of the men demanded.

'The fact that they go all the way up to the roof — if you look closely. That wedge keeping a slit between them was our one hope. Now we've lost it.'

The match dropped to the floor and went out. The three punchers could be heard breathing hard.

'Whatever it costs us,' Al said at length, 'Carson deserved all he got. He wus a no-account heel. I reckon it don't worry me none that I ditched him. Yuh hear that, Gayland?'

There was no answer. Al struck a match hurriedly and with his two cohorts strained their eyes into the darkness.

'I'll be dad-blamed,' one of them breathed, a touch of superstition in his tone. 'Where in hell did they go?'

There was nothing magical about it. At Rod's grip on his arm Bill had moved silently with him, asking no questions. The brief spell of darkness had given them the chance to move some little way from the gunmen and now they were by the wall of the cavern.

'What gives?' Bill murmured, looking at the distant match flame where the three men looked about them.

'We're going to try and find our own way of getting out and be damned to those owl-hooters,' Rod told him. 'It occurs to me that if rock has slipped *downwards*, as it has and crushed Carson, it may have slipped away from a gap in the cavern roof somewheres. I mean taking a look — so let's go.'

In the darkness, whilst they listened to the three distant men arguing among themselves, they found toe- and finger-holds in the rock face and began to climb — presently reaching the first of the natural ledges. Here they paused for a moment regaining their breath and looking about them. Down on the cavern floor a match flared again, a tiny point, and, as it seemed, infinitely distant.

'How do you reckon we can ever discover if there is a gap in the roof?' Bill questioned. 'Seems to me that we're quite a distance from it. Our only way is to climb the central rock pillar where the stuff came down.'

'That's what we're going to do,' Rod agreed. 'We've come up here first to be nearer the roof to see if there's a gap — which as far as I can make out there isn't,' he added after a moment. 'When we climb the central rock pillar we want to be at the *back* of it, away from our pals down there. They'd have heard us if we'd have done it now. So we'll move them on and then go down to the ground again.'

'Move them on? How?'

'Listen,' Rod murmured — and picking up a chunk of rock he hurled it into the blackness. The sound of its falling came echoing back from the further reaches of the cavern.

'They're over there some place!' came a yell from Al. 'Come on!'

Feet shifted and scraped in the gloom

— then far away a match glimmered as the three men began searching.

'That should keep them quiet for a bit,' Rod commented drily; 'and evidently they're dumb enough to fall for that old gag. They probably think we're up there looking for a secret way out. Let's get below.'

He and Bill descended as swiftly and quietly as they could to the cavern floor and, with their sense of direction more or less still clear in their minds, they made for the rear of the central rock pillar and began climbing it. They were half way up when Al and his cohorts began to return.

'Something phony about those two guys,' he commented, from the darkness. 'I'll lay evens they know a way outa this joint an' are double-crossing us. If only it weren't so blamed dark I could deal with 'em pronto.'

'Guess he's right there too,' Bill muttered, climbing silently beside Rod. 'We've no guns if it comes to a showdown, Rod.'

'I'm not worryin' about that. They're in the dark, remember, and that saves us.'

They went on climbing steadily, but there was still nothing but unrelieved blackness overhead. Not the remotest sign of a streak of light.

'Begins to look as though I guessed wrong,' Rod breathed, pausing for a moment and looking about him. 'Mebbe this rockpile is just a cairn or something and has no roof connection. If so we're no better off — '

'Hey, Al!' come a yell from below. 'I've found some wood. An old packin' case or something! In fact there's a lot of em — !' There was the sound of somebody blundering about on the cavern floor and presently a match flickered in the distance.

'Yeah,' came the voice of Al. 'I guess the stuff musta bin left behind by whoever wus last here. We can git a fire out of it anyways an' see what we're doing.'

'Hell,' Bill muttered, as Rod crouched

beside him. 'This ain't going to improve our chances, Rod.'

'If they see us,' Rod answered, 'they'll probably shoot — assuming we are heading for a way out without telling them. The only chance if they start doing that is to pelt 'em with stones and, if possible, get near enough to them to get a gun from one of them — '

He broke off and lay watching intently as the gigantic cavern suddenly became illuminated before a column of flame as Al set the old crates, relic of a long forgotten expedition to the mine, on fire. Smoke ascended too in choking clouds and began to roll along the cavern roof.

'One thing's sure,' Rod said, looking about him in the crimson glow, 'there isn't an outlet in this roof otherwise the smoke would go through it. That saves us a lot of looking. I guess we'd better get down and take our chance.'

He moved preparatory to doing so and then paused as Al's voice below shouted up to him.

'So that's where you've gotten to! What d'yuh figger doin' up there, Gayland?'

Rod shrugged. 'Just struck me there might be a way out, that's all.'

'Yeah? Mighty quiet about it wasn't yuh? Come down here, both uv yuh! I don't trust you outa my sight.'

Al waved his gun so Rod began to descend. As he did so he murmured a few words in Bill's ear.

'Sooner or later, Bill, these three guys are going to wipe us out if they can — not so much for the love of murder but because they're leary of what we might pull on them. They'll get more desperate when they realize there's no way out of this place. Our only hope is to get them first — and to start with we'll have to use our fists.'

'Not much point in it if there's no way out when we've finished, is there?' Bill asked.

'We'll be able to move around in greater safety — and I haven't yet given up hope of getting out. Watch your opportunity.'

172

They reached the base of the cairn and Al stood looking at them grimly.

'Stick over there where I can watch yuh,' he snapped. 'Even if we are shut in here together it don't make us bosom friends!'

Rod glanced beyond Al's tall, whip-cord figure to where the other two men were feeding the burning crates into the flames.

'You're not being so smart, Al,' Rod said. 'What are you trying to do? Suffocate us? How do you imagine the smoke is going to escape?'

'I reckon there's plenty of room fur it without a chimney with all the passages . . .'

Al looked about him speculatively and in that moment Rod acted. He lashed up his clenched right fist in a hammer blow and took the unprepared gunman on the chin. With a gasp of pain he staggered backwards on his heels, overbalanced, and fell to the floor. In an instant he levelled his gun, but not quickly enough. A well-aimed kick from Bill struck him on the wrist and the weapon went flying.

In one dive Rod had seized it, and at the same instant there came the explosion of a gun from the two men tending the fire. Rock chipped out of the floor an inch from Rod's foot. He twirled and fired. One of the men buckled at the knees and collapsed, his gun dropping from his fingers.

'All right, you two,' Rod said curtly. 'It's my party for a change. On your feet, Al. Bill, take that other guy's hardware for yourself. And collect the dead guy's gun too.'

Bill did so and the remaining two gunmen, motioned to stand together, stood with their hands raised, waiting.

'Bit of a waste of time, isn't it?' Al asked sourly. 'Now you've got us what d'you aim to do with us?'

'Make you work!' Rod answered. 'This smoke is drifting slowly in one direction and we've got to find out where. Wherever it's going there must be some kind of opening — so mebbe you did some good by lighting that fire after all . . . Get moving — to the other side of the cavern: that seems to be where the smoke is moving . . . '

★   ★   ★

And whilst the men were entombed Maninza stood before Val in the moonlight with her gun cocked.

'I'm not going to kill you because I've any personal grudge, Miss Kent,' Maninza said. 'Only because I — '

'Hold it,' Val interrupted, thinking swiftly. 'If you kill me you're liable to lose the very thing you're wanting to know about.'

'Meaning — the mine?' The Indian girl sounded suspicious.

'Exactly.' Val knew perfectly well she was telling lies — and taking a desperate chance by so doing — but the longer she postponed her death the better her opportunity of perhaps getting the upper hand later. In fact Maninza herself had provided the idea. She had led the men into a trap, so Val did not see why she herself might not use the same idea.

'Well, well, I'm waiting!' Maninza snapped. 'What about the mine? How much do you know?'

'Everything. Not so long ago I was chasing Dusty Morgan, but I failed to catch him up. In his desperation to get away from me his horse missed its footing and Dusty dropped into Devil's Canyon. I managed to reach him before he died and he told me where the mine is.'

'He did? Why did he particularly tell you? Had you some particular regard for him or something?'

'I was one of his best friends — That's beside the point, isn't it?' Val asked. 'I know where the mine is and I can take you straight to it.'

Maninza shrugged in the moonlight. 'Very well. I've nothing to lose by coming with you — but if you're double-crossing me, Miss Kent, you'll pay for it.'

Val said nothing. She turned to her

horse and mounted it. In a moment or two Maninza was also astride her own mount and the two women rode slowly away from the shelving side of the gully and into the common grey of the foothills.

'In which direction does the mine lie?' Maninza snapped, her gun handy for any emergency.

'At the far end of Devil's Canyon — where Dusty dropped. No more than a couple of miles from here.'

'I never heard of a gold mine in that region,' Maninza mused. 'Still, that doesn't say it can't exist — For your sake, Miss Kent, it had better.'

'If it doesn't,' Val said urgently, 'you can't blame me! I have no guarantee that Dusty was speaking the truth. He may even have been raving with delirium before he died. I know the area he mentioned, so all we can do is hope for the best.'

'I shall want something much more than that. I've been cheated out of my heritage long enough!'

Val said no more. She had paved the way for the inevitable fact that no mine would be discovered, but how much good it would do her she did not know. She had to think of something effective, and quickly, to get the upper hand of Maninza before the site of the mythical mine was reached.

Maninza was wary, however. She kept her eyes almost constantly on Val as she rode — and Val for her part was nearly too weary to think anyway. So much exertion and excitement on top of the man-handling she had received earlier were commencing to tell on her.

It was some ten minutes later when they came to the rugged moonlit terrain which marked the entrance to Devil's Canyon — actually the chasm into which Dusty had plunged from the high rimrock now hidden in the shadows. Val glanced up towards it and gave a little shiver as she recalled the old prospector's dive to destruction.

When they were half way along the canyon Val drew rein and looked about her. Maninza sat watching, one elbow on the saddle-horn.

'From what he told me,' Val said, 'it should be around here. He said the entrance to it was in one of the mountain caves near here. We'd better see what we can find. I've no more idea of the exact spot at the moment than you have.'

Maninza did not say anything though it was plain from her manner that she suspected the whole thing was a trick. She slipped from her mount, motioned Val to do likewise, and they left the animals reined to a rock spur. Then, together, Maninza slightly to the rear with her gun ready, they began moving towards the face of the canyon, surveying as they went the innumerable black ovals in the greyness which marked the entrance to caves.

'Apparently Dusty was not very explicit, Miss Kent,' Maninza remarked drily, as they moved along. 'With all these caves — nearly twenty of them — it might take us several weeks to explore each one of them.'

'Yes, I suppose it might,' Val admitted. 'That's all he had time to say, though, before he died.'

'Suppose I said that I don't believe you?' Maninza snapped, and came to a halt, her gun jammed in Val's back.

Val felt her heart racing again, but she spoke calmly.

'You're jumping to conclusions pretty hastily, aren't you?' she asked. 'We haven't even looked yet. I can't tell you any more than Dusty told me.'

'I don't believe Dusty told you anything,' the Aztec girl breathed. 'In fact I've only your word for it that he's even dead! At this very moment he's probably miles away, laughing in our faces. You've got me here for some reason of your own, Miss Kent, and I think it's time we had a showdown.'

Val turned slowly. Maninza did not stop her. She stood glowering in the moonlight, her mouth a thin line. Val nodded her head towards the rimrock above them.

'If you don't believe Dusty went over to his death come and look at the trail. He must have left hoof-prints behind, and you'll see for yourself where they go out into space.'

Maninza reflected, then to Val's relief she nodded. A little more time was gained.

'Very well, I'll satisfy myself on that,' the Indian girl said. 'Go on — start climbing!'

Fatigued though she was Val obeyed, clawing her way up the rocks steadily with Maninza close behind her. It took them ten minutes of gruelling struggle to reach the rimrock ledge; then they stood up, breathing hard, and looking about them in the pale reflected glow from the moon. Otherwise they were in shadow, which was one advantage which Val was seeking. Up here, with a two hundred foot drop into the canyon, she only needed to catch Maninza unawares for a fraction of a second to be rid of her —

'I'm not standing here all night!'

181

Maninza snapped. 'Where is the horse trail?'

Val began moving, looking intently at the dust of the trail. She had to work by memory to remember the approximate point at which Dusty had plunged over — but presently she came across the marks she wanted, leading down from a higher ledge, down which Dusty had presumably first come.

'Here — plain enough!' Val pointed to the marks and Maninza stooped intently to look.

Instantly Val slammed up her fist, dashing it straight into the Indian girl's face when she bowed forward. She gasped with the sudden blinding impact and Val dived for the gun in Maninza's right hand. She dived too urgently, however, and in her anxiety she missed her grip of the weapon and it went sailing down into the chasm.

Then Maninza had recovered. She whirled round, her hands tearing at Val's shoulders and swinging her forward dizzily. Val lashed out with her foot, cracked it across Maninza's shin, and then tore free of her grip.

In a leap Val jumped to the sloping chasm side from the ledge, intending to get to the bottom and her horse as fast as she could go — but a chunk of stone aimed viciously from Maninza struck her on the back of the head and all but knocked the senses out of her. Sprawling, half conscious, she tumbled against a rock spur and remained there for a moment whilst she recovered.

In a hail of stones and chippings Maninza came tumbling down the slope, stopped herself, then dragged Val to her feet. With vindictive violence she struck Val across the face back and forth. Hurt though she was by the double blow, Val came back to life under it. Her hands flew to Maninza's throat and locked themselves there, her fingers crushing with all the power she possessed.

For a moment or two Val had the advantage. She was a strongly made girl with reasonably tough muscles under her curves, but on this occasion physical weariness was her enemy, and Maninza too had the gift of wriggling and sliding like a snake. She wrenched herself free of the choking grip at length and delivered a shove which sent Val stumbling and rolling helplessly down the slope. She clawed frantically at out-jutting pieces of rock as she went, to break her fall, and finally managed to get a grip on one which brought her head-long drop to a halt. She struggled on to her feet and, pursued by Maninza from above, hurried down to the canyon floor. The Aztec girl fired once with her remaining gun, missed completely, and then apparently gave up the attempt in the dim light.

She caught up with Val as she reached the floor of the canyon, seized her shoulder and dragged her to a stop.

'The fun's over, Miss Kent,' she said grimly. 'I missed you before when I tried to shoot, but I won't this time!'

She snatched out her gun and levelled it. Val threw herself desperately to one side, and at the same moment there came the crack of a shot from somewhere quite close at hand. It stopped Maninza in mid-action. She twirled round; then at a second shot — the fire from which Val saw a dozen yards away near a rock — her revolver fell from her hand and she dropped slowly to her knees. Abruptly she pitched forward on her face and lay still.

Val looked around her in wonder in the moonlight, absorbing the surprising and glorious fact that she had not been touched by Maninza's first bullet. Evidently the fire from the unknown had deflected her aim . . .

Cautiously Val moved forward until she was within a few feet of the prostrate Aztec girl. Prepared for a trick Val inched her way until she was near enough to the girl's dropped gun to seize it. She snatched it up quickly — but Maninza made no movement.

The reason was obvious a moment later. Turning her over Val gazed down in the moonlight upon a neatly drilled hole in the girl's forehead, from which a dark trickle was apparent. The unknown had evidently shot her clean through the brain.

The unknown? Val turned quickly and looked towards the rocks where the saving shots had come from. It surprised her that the owner of the gun had not come forward by now — but there was no sign of anything.

Val left the dead Indian girl where she lay, and, gun in hand, advanced towards the rock where her salvation had come from. She gave a gasp of surprise when she beheld a prone figure, breathing but only half conscious, covered in dirt and dried blood.

'Dusty!' she cried, dropping on her knees and catching at his shoulders. 'Dusty, it's you!'

He opened his eyes in the moonlight and gazed at her. His lips parted in a slight grin over his toothless gums.

'Yeah, kid, sure it's me,' he whispered. 'I-I did my best with my hardware, I guess — Did it work?'

'You saved my life!' Val told Dusty urgently. 'Maninza was all set to kill me and your shots finished her. You got her right in the head.'

'Yeah? Think — uv that.' The old prospector chuckled raspingly. 'Only goes ter show — I can shoot even if I am dyin' — '

'Who says you are?' Val demanded. 'You've got me to help you now — Hang on a minute while I get my water bottle. It's in my saddle-bag.'

She hurried away — and returned a few moments later, unscrewing the bottle stopper. The water brought a little more life back to the old man. He lay breathing hard as Val's arm held his neck and shoulders.

'How on earth did you get here?' she asked curiously. 'The last I saw of you you'd plunged over the rimrock there — just about this point.'

'The last *you* saw of me?' the old man repeated. 'Sweet sufferin' catfish, yuh mean it was *you* who was a-followin me hell fur leather?'

'Sure it was. I shouted to you but evidently you didn't hear me.'

Dusty spent a few moments cursing himself; then he stirred a little and spoke again out loud.

'I dropped at the bottom of the slope there, gal, an' my cayuse wandered off some place. I cracked my shin, I think, and cut several good-sized chunks outa myself. Not bein' able to move hardly, an' weak too from the beatin' I took from Carson and his boys, I'd figgered I'd just haveta lie an' die. I hadn't got me gun either with which I might signal. It were took from me long ago — '

'But you fired a gun to save me,' Val pointed out puzzled.

'Yeah — I'm a-comin' to that. I was coiled up in them rocks over there' — he nodded to the sloping side of the canyon — 'and half asleep when somethin' dropped an' hit me mighty hard on th' forehead. I thought it were a chunk uv rock at first — then I found it was a thirty-two. That woke me up, I guess, but my leg gave me too much hell to move it. So I just lay a-watchin', an' I saw you and Maninza come down th' slope some distance frum me. Didn't take me long t'see that Maninza was on the prod fur you . . . so I took care of her. I guess that's all there is.'

'It's enough — and it's marvellous,' Val said quickly. 'My job is to give you a hand to Maninza's pinto back there. My own horse is there too. And let's have no more talk about dying. You're tough enough to stand a broken leg, surely?'

'Sure thing, gal. Just kiddin', that's all.'

'I want to get on the move as soon as possible,' Val added, and as Dusty looked at her questioningly she outlined the predicament in which she had left Rod.

'I don't like the sound uv that,' the old man said grimly. 'Carson and Rod Gayland locked up together, y'say? If they ever can get out I'll gamble they don't come out together. Like as not

189

they'll have shot each other by now — An' what makes yuh think it'll be so easy to open that mine door?'

'I don't think it will be easy, but explosives ought to do it, surely? I can get some gelignite in the town — Or better still I can tell the sheriff all about it and have him do the job; then he can rope in Carson and his boys the moment they come out into the open.'

'Yeah — mebbe,' Dusty said dubiously. 'It's that door to th' mine I'm thinkin' uv. I've seen dozens of 'em scattered around Arizony and most of 'em are deep sunk in th' bedrock an' can't be shifted. Remember, gal, them doors were put on to guard gold — so yuh can be pretty sure explosives won't shift 'em.'

'Then — then what *can* we do?' Val moved helplessly and spread her hands in the moonlight. 'I've got to make some kind of effort to save Rod — and quickly too. There's no guarantee how long he can last out for air in that confined space.'

'Yore ways off your horse there, gal! None of them mines is confined. They go back miles into th' mountains — ' The old man broke off as a thought seemed to strike him. He wriggled into a sitting position and breathed hard, holding the girl's shoulder for support. 'Whereabouts did yuh say this partic'lar mine is?' he demanded.

'About two miles from here. When you reach the top end of this canyon you bear to the right — '

'And move to the other side of this mountain range here?'

'Uh-huh,' Val agreed, after thinking. 'I suppose you do.'

'Then yuh can bet your boots, lass, that that mine goes into this range here. They all do, more or less, since it's only in the mountains where gold is found. Then the Aztecs usta take it out and store it somewheres for safety, sealin' off the mines with them big doors — What I'm drivin' at is that there might be a back way into the mine where Rod Gayland an' the rest uv 'em are stuck. Up through them caves there.'

Dusty looked at the cliff face and then sighed. 'Trouble is I couldn't never make it,' he said bitterly. 'Not with me leg like this.'

There was silence for a moment, then Val said:

'In any case, Dusty, there are dozens of cave mouths up there. How do you suppose the right one could ever be located?'

'I dunno. Just risk it, I guess, an' hope for the best.'

'With no torches, ropes, or anything? Not me. I'll try the easier way and see if the sheriff can't have the door blown in. We're going right back into town this moment, get you fixed up, then I'm coming back with the sheriff.'

'And drop from exhaustion on the way, gal?' the old man asked. 'Yore out on yuh feet right now only yuh won't admit it.'

'The ride will give me a rest,' she said. 'Come on — I'll give you a hand.'

Dusty made an effort and struggled with difficulty on to his sound foot. With his arm about Val's neck he was able at last to stand up, then he transferred his hand to the nearby rock to support himself.

'I'll fetch the horses,' Val said, and went off towards them wearily . . .

7

Evidently Dusty was a better judge of Val's condition than she was herself, for by the time Hell's Acres was reached she was nearly falling asleep from utter weariness. She did manage to hold up long enough to reach the sheriff's home on the edge of the darkened town — but before he had come to open the door she had slumped in a faint in the porchway.

Dusty unable to get off his horse unaided, sat and waited — and presently an oil-lamp with its glimmering flame appeared behind the screen door. The door opened and Sheriff Hawkins looked out into the night, then in amazement at the body at his feet.

'What in hell — ' he burst out, stooping; then Dusty's voice reached him.

'Yuh'd best take the gal inside an'

have yuh wife look after her, sheriff, then come back fur me. I've a broken leg an' the energy uv a kitten.'

'But what's it all about?' Hawkins demanded. 'An' at this hour of night. I was asleep — '

'Then git the sleep outa yuh and prepare fur some hard work. You're sure going to get some.'

The sheriff hesitated and then nodded. He picked Val up in his arms and carried her inside. Presently Dusty was also being helped into the living room and the sheriff and his wife listened to the old man's story whilst Val slowly recovered on the sofa.

'So that's the way it is?' Hawkins asked, and went over to the door for his cross-over gun-belts. 'Okay, I'll get out to that mine pronto and see what I can do — As for Carson I've bin wanting to pin something on him for long enough. My wife'll take care of you two,' he added. 'Right now I'm going to rustle me some men together.'

He departed urgently and got his

horse from the stable. To summon together the men he needed he used the usual procedure in an emergency — smote fiercely on the triangle which hung from a gibbet in the high street. Stampedes, posses, and other matters which demanded the populace should know about them were always prefaced in this fashion.

Sure enough, as Sheriff Hawkins stood beside the still humming triangle and looked about him in the moonlight he beheld upper windows opening, and here and there in the distance men and women appearing on the boardwalks in their night attire.

'I want help,' he stated briefly — which he knew was enough explanation with his trustworthy reputation. 'There's some men trapped back in an Aztec mine — some of 'em crooks. I ain't sayin' who they are but I've gotta dig 'em out. Only way seems to be with gelignite. Grab it, somebody, from the powder stores. As many more of you as want had better come with me.'

Altogether, in about ten minutes, he had collected perhaps a dozen men, including his two deputies, one of whom had made it his business to collect the gelignite.

'Okay,' Hawkins said, as he surveyed the party. 'That's about enough. If any of you women' — he looked towards the boardwalk where a considerable crowd had gathered — 'want to do a good turn y'might go and help my wife. She's got Miss Kent and an injured prospector on her hands, an' it ain't an easy job.'

'Miss Kent!' ejaculated the loud voice of Ma Gunthorpe, though she herself was hidden in gloom. 'I'll git me over to your place right now, sheriff. That gal's my partic'lar charge. I've bin a-wonderin' where she'd gotten to.'

'Okay,' the sheriff said. 'Let's go, boys!'

He spurred his big sorrel and with the men behind him swept up the moonlit high street and out of the town. As fast as they could go they thundered their mounts down the main trail, its powdery dust shining white in the glimmer of the moon. Sheriff Hawkins had a pretty good idea from Val's description whereabouts the mine lay — but even so it was a good hour after he and the men had left Hell's Acres before they stumbled upon the gully they wanted and found the massive copper door at the end of it.

The sheriff slid from his horse and hurried towards the barrier. His two deputies lighted flares and in silence they all stood looking at the impregnable rectangle.

'I guess it'd take a coupla good earthquakes to blow that dad-blamed thing out uv its frame,' Hawkins said at last, his hat cuffed up on his forehead. 'Anyways, we'll do our best. Better see if they can hear us inside first, so's we can warn 'em to get clear.'

He picked up a heavy rock and banged on the door with all his strength. The noise it gave back was rather like hitting the lid of a coffin. Though he tried several times there was no response from within.

'Either dead or they can't hear us,' he said finally. 'Okay, Jake, get those sticks bedded down and we'll see what we can do.'

Jake nodded and set to work, the remaining men helping him. It was a long job, and a dangerous one, but since they had all the necessary tackle with them they did it thoroughly. Finally the fuse was lighted and the men got clear, taking their horses, and sought shelter behind the highest rocks they could find.

Some seconds later the earth opened in a blinding flash of flame and a detonation which rumbled across the silent pasturelands. Rocks, dust and earth went sailing high against the moon and the waiting men were pelted with debris as it rained back to earth.

The disturbance over, they hurried forward to investigate, and then looked at each other grimly. The door was still there, as firmly fastened as ever. The rocks around it had been blown to hell, and a smoking hole lay in front of it — but that was all.

'Damn!' Sheriff Hawkins swore, and spat.

'Say, do you figger we might dig through that hole and so under the door?' Jake suggested.

'I reckon not. We'll only meet up with bedrock at this depth, an' even assumin' we could get through it we'd still have to go upwards to get inside. We couldn't do it.'

'Only one way then,' one of the men said. 'Do as Old Timer suggested an' see if there's a back way in by those caves . . . '

Hawkins nodded slowly. 'Yeah. We can try anyways, though I don't hold out much hope. Okay, let's go . . . '

He and his men moved towards their horses, and at about the same moment a solitary man was also moving towards the Hawkins' home on the outside of Hell's Acres. Swarthy, grim-faced in the moonlight, he had his heavy .45 in his hand and was hell-bent on business. Not far away his horse was tethered.

When he reached the sheriff's little wooden home he stood looking at the lamplight on the curtains of the living room. Here the window was quite small and of the ordinary up and down variety. For a long time the solitary gunhawk considered, surveying the calmness of the night and making sure he was alone — then he began to advance slowly, reached the window, and found it was at the level of his shoulder.

'Couldn't be better,' he murmured — and with sudden impact he smashed the glass of the window with his gun and pointed it through the curtains into the room beyond.

The little assembly in the lamplight stared at him in alarm, motionless, too astonished to make a move. The gunman took in the scene quickly. On the couch lay Val, sipping something from a bowl. In a chair, the much bandaged Dusty Morgan was also drinking soup. Behind them were two women — the sheriff's wife and the ample figure of Ma Gunthorpe.

'Well, quite a nice little family gathering!' the gunman commented; then still keeping his gun levelled he clambered into the room. 'Don't any of yuh move if yuh want to stay healthy!'

'What's the meaning of this, Tom Callahan?' Ma Gunthorpe demanded, her eyes glinting. 'I never thought you was the low-down sort of critter who'd pull a gun on women even if you do truck around with that no-account heel Drew Carson!'

'Right now, Ma, I'm only interested in one person,' Callahan retorted. 'This old guy in the chair here.' He went over to Dusty and looked at him fixedly.

'I kind uv figgered that wus it,' the old man said bitterly. 'I draw gun-hawks more'n a cayuse draws flies.'

'The sheriff shot his mouth off back in town,' Callahan went on. 'Told everybody that you wus here — but I reckon nobody had th' sense t' take advantage of it 'cept me. I don't know where Carson is — an' I don't care — so I don't need ter tell him. I'm acting on me own, see? Right off me own mark . . . Where's that mine, old timer? Tell me that an' you ain't got no more to worry about.'

At the back of Dusty the women moved restlessly. The gunman's weapon levelled at them.

'Take it easy back there. Don't make it that I haveta drill yuh!'

'Better be sure you don't get drilled first yourself, Tom!' Ma Gunthorpe snapped. 'You don't suppose we're just going to stand here an' watch you get away with it, do you?'

'Yeah — I do, 'cos I think yuh've more sense'n try anything crazy — All right, you!' Callahan snapped, as Dusty sat looking at him grimly. 'On your feet!'

'Can't be done,' the old man responded. 'I've got a broken leg.'

'Yeah? That's just too bad — but it still leaves yuh one leg to git around on.

Come on — *move!*'

Callahan hesitated no longer. Brushing aside the bowl of soup in Dusty's hands he hauled the old man upwards by one hand knotted in his shirt front. He stood swaying on his one foot, supported by the gunman's grip.

'Leave him be!' Val snapped. 'Can't you see that he — '

'You shut up!' Callahan flared at her; then swinging back to Dusty — 'Start hoppin' — outside. You an' me are goin' places. I don't aim to let everybody know about this mine when you start talkin'. Hurry it up!'

With the gun in his back Dusty had no alternative. With the gunman holding on to him he hopped out to the porch and from it across the yard. Once this far Callahan whistled his horse and lifted Dusty up to the saddle, swinging up behind him. Just in time Callahan turned with his revolver to see Ma Gunthorpe with a rifle.

'Better not, Ma!' he shouted. 'I reckon yore liable to hit Dusty instead uv me if yuh monkey around with that thing.'

Ma Gunthorpe hesitated, her lips compressed. In silence she watched the gunman whirl his mount round and then spur it into the night. The sheriff's wife came hurrying out and stood for a moment watching the horse vanish with its two riders.

'So he got away with it, huh?' she demanded. 'Why didn't you take a risk and shoot?'

'The risk was too great, I guess. I didn't dare — '

'Get me a horse quickly!' came Val's urgent voice, and she came out on to the porchway. 'My own's too tired, I think. I want one that can move fast — '

'But what d'you suppose you can do?' Ma Gunthorpe demanded, staring at her in the moonlight. 'You're all in, gal. Get back in there and rest — '

'There's no time for that, Ma! Don't you realize, that Dusty may be killed if somebody doesn't try and help him?

There only seems to be me who can do it — A horse, please! Hurry it up! Don't worry about me. I'm rested enough by now.'

This was a definite exaggeration on Val's part, but the knowledge of Dusty's danger gave her unexpected vitality. The sheriff's wife took her at her word and hurried down to the stable from the porch. In another moment or two she brought a ready-saddled mare into view.

Val returned from the living-room, her kerchief knotted at her throat and one of Maninza's .32s in her belt.

'I reckon yore takin' a big chance, gal,' Ma Gunthorpe said anxiously. 'Wish I could come with you, but I'm past ridin' at my age.'

Val did not say anything. She went down the steps, climbed into the horse's saddle, and then rode swiftly away in the direction the gunhawk had taken . . .

By this time he was quite a mile and a half away and riding hard. Dusty made no effort to move. Indeed he could not. His broken leg, heavily bandaged and in splints, was sufficient reason for him sitting immovable.

'I reckon this should do,' the gunhawk said at length, when they had come to a bend in the trail. 'I mean to find out where that gold of yourn is even if I have to break your other leg to match!'

He dragged the horse to a standstill and looked about him. Then he started the animal off again, left the trail, and rode over the pastureland until he came to the first outcroppings of the foothill forest. Here, well screened by the dense trees, he stopped and dismounted.

'Down yuh git!' he ordered, and half dragged the old man from the saddle. 'Now, let's get one thing straight. I'm not goin' t'pull my punches. Either you tell me what I want to know — an' guide me to where the mine is — or I'll take yuh apart by inches. I know yuh've been threatened that way before and stood up to it, in Carson's shack f'r instances, but I don't aim to tire yuh out slowly. I want the answer right now . . . '

'Okay,' Dusty muttered. 'Yuh can have it.'

The gunhawk looked at him suspiciously. 'Yuh mean yore tellin' me everythin' without a struggle?'

'Yeah. What strength have I got left to keep on standin' up to th' punishment you blasted owl-hooters keep dishin' out? I guess my life's a durned sight more valuable to me than gold. I'll take yuh to the mine an' put an end to this chasin' and beatin' up I keep runnin' inter.'

'OK,' Callahan muttered. 'I guess that's good enough fur me.'

*   *   *

High on the rimrock from which Dusty had plunged on his horse earlier in the night, Sheriff Hawkins and his party made their way along in single file, the horses testing every step on the

208

treacherous rock. They had already investigated three caves and found they led into a dead end — now they were bent on exploring a further group of them a quarter of a mile distant and lying at the level of the trail so they could be easily reached.

'Say,' one of the deputies said suddenly, raising his head, 'do you smell smoke?'

Hawkins sniffed the night wind as he rode cautiously along, then at length he nodded. He stopped his horse and hipped round in the saddle, gazing back in the moonlight at the dark tangle of the forest nestling in the distant foothills.

'Smells like wood,' he said. 'I thought for a moment it might be the forest that had caught fire — but that's dead enough. Seems to be blowin' downwind some place.'

'Not far ahead either,' one of the men said. 'Better take care what we're doin' — could even be Carson and his boys around a campfire or sump'n.'

Hawkins nodded and said no more. He urged his mount on again gently, and with the advance the smell of smoke grew noticeably stronger. Finally Hawkins gave an ejaculation.

'It's comin' from that cave ahead of us. I can even see it — faint-like — against the moonlight.'

He was right. When the cave mouth was reached thin streamers of smoke were visible dissipating into the night. The men looked into the cave, then at each other.

'Ain't a campfire,' a deputy said. 'Black as a blasted tomb in there.'

'Could be a signal, though,' Hawkins decided. 'Wouldn't be the first time that folks entombed have used smoke to show where they are. Let's take a look . . . Curly, get those torches lit up.'

The oiled brands were duly lighted and to the accompaniment of flickering flames the men rode into the cave, fastened their horses to jutting rock-spurs, and then looked around them. It was not very long before one of them spied a narrow fissure in the back of the cave, about twelve inches across and about five feet high.

'I guess we might just squeeze through,' the sheriff decided. 'Do us no harm to try, anyways. You, Larry, stay here and watch the horses — an' for any trouble that might develop. Looks like we may have gotten on to the guys who got themselves shut in the mine.'

He moved to the gap, squashed himself through it, and then took one of the torches. The flame illumined a narrow, roughly bored passage, obviously the work of volcanic activity. It demanded that Hawkins and the men behind him go on their knees to reach the end of it. All the time they went smoke wafted past them, not enough to sting their eyes or set them coughing, but enough to create the unmistakable odour of burning.

Abruptly the tunnel opened out into a small-sized cavern. They began moving across it, then stopped as they came to a massive fissure stretching right across the cavern floor in a zig zag line. In width it was no than a foot at its widest point and through it smoke was drifting lazily.

Immediately Hawkins went down on his knees and shouted, into the crack.

'Hey there! Anybody down there?'

There was a long interval as his voice went rolling into echoes; then from far away came an answer, muffled by intervening rock which baffled the sound-waves.

'Two of us! Rod Gayland and Bill Tandrill . . . Who's there?'

'Sheriff Hawkins. What happened to Carson? And the others?'

'Carson got himself killed — One of the boys I had to shoot before he shot me.' There was a long pause, then Rod's voice added, 'We've been wandering in the underground hell knows how long. We started off with two of Carson's men. They were ahead of us and slipped down a shaft. Killed, I reckon. It saved Bill and me droppin' down after them, any ways.'

'Where are you now?'

'We've worked our way round the edge of the shaft on a narrow ledge. No guarantee how long it will hold us. Bits of it keep breaking away. If it goes — we go, down the shaft. And we won't come up again. There's an old wooden door in front of us but we can't budge it.'

'Rock fall behind it holding it fast, y'mean?'

'No. Doesn't feel like rock. Door budges a bit, but I think some wooden props have dropped across it and jammed it. If you can get to it and pull 'em away we might do it.'

'Can't be done,' Hawkins shouted. 'This crack I'm talkin' through isn't more'n a foot or so wide. We're all too big to squeeze. Needs a child, or sump'n. Guess I'd better send back to town for a kid we can lower through. How long can you hold out on that ledge?'

'Not long,' came Rod's urgent voice. 'And for God's sake don't use any explosive or this ledge will give way.'

'Hang on,' Hawkins shouted. 'I'll do everything I can — '

He turned swiftly and gave his orders. Immediately one of the men turned and sped back as rapidly as possible whence he and the others had come, *en route* for a hell-for-leather ride into town to find a child who could get through the fissure.

Hawkins turned back to the gap, took one of the torches, and dropped it into the blackness below. It struck rock some forty feet down and broke up into brief but brilliant flame.

'Suffering cats,' Hawkins whispered, as his men peered with him. 'Take a look at that.'

The glare was sufficient for them to see that a half caved-in shaft lay below. Part of the way up it, hanging sheer into space, was a solitary prop which had evidently slipped out of the shaft's underpinnings in the general collapse. It lay right across a massive wooden door, jamming it.

'I reckon that if we could get a rope

around that prop and git all of us pulling we could shift it,' one of the deputies said. 'Only the end of it's buried in rock. But when that door opens those guys are likely to step right out into space. Then there's the problem of how we get 'em through this narrow crack.'

'We don't, yuh bonehead,' Hawkins snapped. 'We'll blast this crack wide enough to get 'em through with ropes around 'em — but we can't blast *first* because that ledge they're on'll collapse. Problem's going to be to get a rope around that prop. It'll haveta be knotted round its middle. Not a thing you can lasso from this angle and in this narrow space.'

There was silence for a moment, then one of the deputies spoke.

'It means that if we can get hold of a kid from somewheres — an' there ain't many mothers I know uv who'll let their kid do a stunt like this — he's gotta swing in space held by us until he's gotten a rope round that beam.'

'Yeah,' Hawkins agreed grimly. 'Then he's gotta stay there until those guys break free so's he can swing across an' give 'em ropes to fasten around themselves. They'll never git hold of a rope any other way. No use fastening it to the beam for them to reach to 'cos that beam's goin' to drop in the shaft once it's pulled free.' Hawkins breathed hard. 'Only hope is we can get a kid with nerve enough to do it.'

He waited for a moment, thinking, then communicated his discoveries and intentions to Rod and Bill. Rod's muffled answer came back at length.

'Haveta leave it to you, sheriff — but for God's sake hurry it up! This ledge is passing out under us!'

Hawkins said nothing. There was nothing he *could* say. Never in his life had he felt so powerless . . . He sat back on his heels to wait, and whilst he did so the lone rider who had volunteered to race back into town was speeding with demoniacal urgency through the moonlight, dust clouding the flying feet

216

of the horse as he hurtled down the trail.

To his surprise he saw the dim shape of an approaching horseman when he was half way to Hell's Acres. It being too late to dodge from sight in the bright moonlight he drew his gun in readiness as he thundered on. In this region one had to be prepared for an enemy at every turn . . . Only it was not an enemy. It was Val who came riding up swiftly.

'Miss Kent!' the rider cried in surprise, drawing rein. 'Say, what are — '

'You seen Dusty Morgan and a gunhawk named Callahan riding with him?' she demanded. 'Both on one horse?'

'No, but then I — '

'They came part of the way here; I followed their trail. Then I lost it. I've got to find them. That old man's in danger of his life. You'd better help me — '

'I've no time.' The puncher made his

urgency clearer, and then caught the girl's arm. 'Look, miss, those two men are in deadly danger every minute I waste. Do yuh suppose there's anything *you* could do about it and cut time in half?'

Val drummed her hands on the saddle-horn in desperate indecision.

'For heaven's sake, what am I to *do*?' she cried. 'Dusty in peril of his life on one hand, and Rod in danger on the other. Naturally Rod's first as far as I'm concerned, but what if I'm wasting time? Do you think I can get through this gap you speak of?'

'I reckon so. You're mighty slender build — Try, anyways,' the puncher urged. 'If it fails y'can do your best to pick up Dusty Morgan's trail afterwards.'

'Mebbe,' Val sighed. 'I seem to have lost it — All right, let's go,' she broke off quickly, and spurred her mare.

Immediately the puncher swung round to follow her, thereafter taking the lead. In the space of perhaps ten minutes they had reached the cave. In another five they had gained the fissure where Hawkins and his men were waiting anxiously, torches flaming around them.

'So soon — ?' the sheriff exclaimed, astonished — then he gave a start as he saw Val, pale-faced but determined.

'Thought it might be easier,' the puncher explained. 'T'say nothing of quicker. Rod Gayland means a lot to Miss Kent here: more than to a kid anyways. She's willing to have a try.'

'Get the lariats,' Hawkins ordered; then motioned to the girl. 'See if you can get into that crack, Miss Kent.'

She nodded and went over to it. By easing herself gradually into it she found she could just make it. She remained for a moment, supporting herself by her arms stretched on the rock on either side of the gap and her body dangling in emptiness.

'OK?' Hawkins asked, and she nodded, pulling herself up to the level again.

'Yes, I can just about do it.'

'You know what's happened?'

'I guess so,' Val assented. 'Lucky for you you noticed smoke, otherwise you might have gone on searching for ever.'

'Yeah . . . ' Hawkins looked up as two men came hurrying back with ropes. 'I guess the smoke's escaping through niches in the rocks. Pity is them niches aren't big enough to let a body through — '

He broke off as from far away there came a cry.

'Hey there, sheriff! Half this ledge has just gone — If you don't act fast we shan't be here much longer!'

Val motioned quickly. 'Come on — get me fixed up. What do you propose doing?'

'Making a cradle you can sit in and we'll lower you down.'

She nodded and watched intently as a big loop was made in the end of the tough lariat cord. Moving to the gap she slipped the rope about her, down as far as the back of her knees, then began to lower herself. Two of the men dropped lighted torches below to

220

illuminate the scene — then Hawkins gave the signal. Three of the powerful cow-punchers held the rope, paying it out very gently.

'Carry on,' Val instructed, when she had disappeared as far as her head. 'And don't forget to hand down the rope I need to fasten around that prop! I don't want to be left hanging like a fish on a line!'

With that she vanished and the rope slid lower. Hawkins threw himself on his face, peering into the void to give orders. The men behind him sweated and strained as the rope took the girl's full weight.

Val dropped by degrees, twirling in the abyss, the whole mass of the caved-in shaft turning in spirals about her. She caught at the second rope as it dangled beside her and waited until she had dropped to the level of the ancient door. Then she shouted up for a halt to be made and swung herself gently to and fro until she was able to grip the fallen prop.

Keeping control of her movements with difficulty, she clawed her way along the prop until she reached its centre. Quickly she drew the rope around it and made a triple knot — then she swung away again and shouted.

'Pull away! Up to you now!'

The rope holding her was transferred to a rock spur so two men alone could hang on to it. The remaining men threw all their strength into dragging on the rope which help the prop. At an angle, because of the ledge, their leverage was not as good as they might have wished, but nevertheless the prop began to move slightly as they tugged.

Val sat watching, the rope cutting painfully into her thighs, the flickering torches giving a dim view of the proceedings. She noticed now that the face of the shaft which contained the door went upwards sheer for nearly twenty feet and then became broken, from which source the smoke started by the burning crates far away in the underground had evidently come.

'Once more!' Val cried. 'Hard as you can — !'

The sweating men above hesitated for a moment and then tugged with every vestige of their strength. The prop gave. It pulled free of its bed of rock and overbalanced. Instantly the men had to release the rope as tremendous weight pulled upon it. The prop went tumbling down into the abyss, leaving the door free.

'Rod!' Val shouted hoarsely. 'Take care when you open the door or you'll step into space!'

'OK,' came his voice; and then there was the creaking and tearing of wood as the door gave way and went sailing down below. Rod became dimly visible in the flickering light, with Bill behind him. They both stopped dead on the edge of the rim, staring in horrified amazement at Val swinging in space.

'Ropes!' she yelled — and two came snaking down instantly.

She grabbed them and once again began her pendulum movement across the gap, until at length her momentum took her far enough for Rod to grasp her whilst Bill took the ropes from her.

'For God's sake, Val, what sort of a risk is this you're taking?' Rod demanded. 'If that rope snaps — '

'It won't — I hope.' She gave him rather an impudent smile. 'It was you or me for it, Rod. You didn't stand a chance, so I took this risk to help you out — and also to prove that gold isn't the only thing I think about. Maybe I'm more the girl you used to know when we first met?'

'Yeah — Yeah, sure you are.' Rod looked at her in wonder as he still held her.

'Tie those ropes around you and wait until they can haul you up,' she instructed. 'They'll have to blast the fissure wider so you can fit through.'

'Why don't you stop here, too? Tell them to let you go. I can hold on to you.'

'No need — and it's too risky. You might overbalance when the rope holding me was released, then where would we be? Don't worry about me. I'll have myself dragged free and we'll talk again later when you're safe up above . . . There's Dusty Morgan too! We've got to find him, Rod. A gunman by the name of Callahan has got him and I shudder to think what may happen to the old boy . . . '

'We'll find him,' Rod said grimly, then he suddenly kissed the girl and released her. Smiling a little he watched her go swinging up to the gap in the dim light of the torches.

8

After half an hour's riding — a far longer journey than he had any real need to take, but which gave him the chance to recover his strength a little in the cool night air — Dusty Morgan came within sight of the little-used trail where lay his skilfully hidden bonanza. He glanced over his shoulder at Callahan.

'OK, this is where we stop. Yuh'll haveta lift me down if I'm to show yuh.'

Callahan drew the horse to a halt and dismounted. He hauled the old prospector down from the saddle and supported him as he hopped on one foot.

'Bit further along,' Dusty said. 'Gimme a hand . . . '

He covered about a hundred yards and then paused, pointing into the distance of the trail where it lost itself in moonlight.

'See that needle uv rock, mebbe half a mile on?' the old man asked, and Callahan nodded as he glanced briefly.

'I reckon that's it. I can't make it that far; the ground's too rough. Go an' see fur yuhself. I guess I can't git away with this leg uv mine.'

Callahan reflected briefly, twirling his gun in his fingers; then deciding that Dusty was speaking the truth he hurried forward swiftly along the trail. The old man watched him go, his toothless mouth creasing in a grin — In a few seconds the thing Dusty had planned happened.

The gunman hurried straight across the gap where the bonanza lay and his weight sent him crashing through the branches and leaves into the depths below. Immediately Dusty hopped back to the horse, clawed his way up into the saddle, then rode the animal forward. As he went he unfastened the lariat from the saddle horn, noosed it, then swung it gently over his head.

He brought the horse to a standstill

at the very edge of the gap. Sure enough Callahan's clawing hands presently appeared as he struggled to drag himself up. It was impossible for him to use his gun as his grip was needed to stop him falling back into the hole.

'Enjoyin' yuhself?' the old man asked, with a dry chuckle.

'Yuh dirty blasted twister!' the gunman spat. 'Yuh knew this trap were here — !'

'Sure I did. Weren't no other way I could think uv to git yuh where I wanted yuh!'

Callahan muttered something, then struggled upwards in the moonlight. Dusty waited until he had got on his knees, then he whirled the rope suddenly. It dropped round the astonished gunman and drew tight, pinning his arms to his sides. Before he could realize what had happened he was flung from his feet as the horse started forward and thereafter he was dragged behind it, torn and lashed by barbs of scrub-grass and sharp-edged rocks.

'For God's sake, stop!' he shrieked. 'Yore cuttin' me to ribbons!'

'Sure am,' Dusty agreed implacably, glancing back at him. 'Just happens t'be your hard luck that yore takin' a beatin' fur all the things Carson done ter me! I may have a broken pin but I can fight back in other ways — an' I'm durned well going to!'

He gave the horse its head. Pounded, battered, half senseless, Callahan was dragged and torn onwards along the ground, his shirt and pants slashed into streamers, blood trickling from a dozen slashes and cuts. At the end of a mile of anguish when the very edge of the foothill forest had been reached, Dusty came to a halt and allowed the groaning man to lie prone in the cool grass.

'Mebbe that'll teach yuh not to go around scarin' women and proddin' old men,' Dusty said. 'Yore no nearer that bonanza uv mine, an' yuh never will be!'

'Yeah?' a voice asked coldly. 'What makes yuh think so?'

Astounded, Dusty twirled round in the saddle. In the shadows of the trees nearby two men were standing — one tall and thin and the other shorter and more powerfully built. Both of them seemed to be almost in rags, but one held a gun steadily.

'Surprised?' asked the tall one, coming forward. 'If so I'm as surprised as you are. Reckon there must be somethin' in coincidence. I'm Al Lemming, one of Carson's right-hand men. I guess Carson's dead right now, so that makes me top man.'

A memory stirred in the prospector's mind. 'Y-Y'mean yore one of them guys who got shut in the mine with Rod Gayland an' the rest uv 'em?'

'Yeah. The dirty critter — Gayland I mean — ditched us. We fell down a shaft, but I reckon it did us some good. We found a way out by an underground tunnel which brought us out not quarter of a mile away. I reckon Gayland thinks we're dead. I'll even gamble he's still tryin' ter find his way outa the maze with that fat jigger uv a Bill Tandrill. That fool missed seein' I had a second gun when he frisked me . . . Anyways, it's lucky we heard yuh talkin'. Saves us a lot of trouble comin' gunnin' fur yuh.' Al moved over to where Callahan lay prostrate and groaning. Reaching down with one hand he unfastened the rope from about him and dragged him to his feet.

'An' what happened ter you?' he demanded acidly. 'Tryin' somethin' on yuh own, huh, without waitin' fur any uv us to git free and share yuh infurmation?'

'He figgered he could sidetrack th' lot uv yuh and git me to show him my bonanza,' Dusty said. 'I guess this is how he finished up. I rough-rided him.'

'Yeah,' Al said venomously. 'Yuh always wus a two-timer, Callahan, but from now on yuh won't be no more, I guess — '

He fired once — twice — three times. The hapless Callahan stood motionless for a moment, a ragged, blood-streaked figure, then he dropped heavily into the grass and remained still. The second gunman cast a glance at his ruthless henchman.

'That settles that,' Al said. 'If I'd have had my way I'd have cleaned up this critter long ago. I guess Carson was too soft-hearted in some things — ' He swung to Dusty. 'As fur you, git off that horse.'

'Nothin' doin', feller. I've a broken leg.'

'I said git off!' Al slammed out his fist and the old prospector reeled helplessly from the saddle and dropped heavily. He lay wincing at the violence of the pain in his shin. Before he had the chance to recover himself he was dragged upwards.

'Get this,' Al said deliberately. 'Plenty uv guys have monkeyed around with tryin' to find out where your mine is an' yuh've ditched th' lot uv 'em. I don't play the game the soft-hearted way. I'm takin' yuh for a ride like you gave Callahan, broken leg or otherwise, unless yuh talk.'

Dusty shook his head dumbly. 'I ain't speakin'. You can kill me first!'

'Kill yuh after, yuh mean. Yore no use ter me, dead. What's it t'be?'

Dusty did not answer. With a growl of fury Al whirled round his fist and knocked the old man sprawling to the ground again. He lay where he had fallen, hardly stirring as he realized the rope which had bound Callahan was now being fastened round the ankle of his sound leg. The cold, cruel voice of Al floated down to him again.

'Ready fur the ride, pardner? Or are yuh goin' ter talk?'

'Yuh can git ter hell!' Dusty spluttered back.

Al wasted no further time. He leapt to the saddle of the horse, his henchman jumping up behind him. Swinging the horse round Al set it speeding along the uneven ground, the hapless figure of Dusty bouncing and bumping in the rear. He screamed once, but that was all. It was his silence thereafter which finally made Al slow down. Puzzled, he reined the horse and dropped from the saddle, going back to where the old prospector lay prostrate in the dust.

'Hell blast it, he's dead!' Al got up from an examination of the old man's body. 'Hit his head on a chunk uv rock or sump'n. Guess that washes it up . . . '

The second gunman was silent, then he spoke bitterly.

'Yuh damned fool, Al! Why couldn't yuh have used something less tough? What good's the old critter to us now he's passed out fur good? We ain't never goin' ter find that gold now!'

'He might have a plan or sump'n in his pockets,' Al said, and went quickly through Dusty's pockets — without result.

'Smart, ain't yuh?' the second gunman demanded.

'Aw, shut up! Lemme think . . . ' He stood brooding for a while, rolling himself a cigarette meanwhile. He lighted it and thought some more, flicking the match out of his fingers.

'Well, do we durned well stand here all night?' the second gunman demanded finally. 'I've had about enough even if you haven't. I reckon we can write off that bonanza as lost.'

'I'm just thinkin',' Al mused. 'I reckon Dusty must ha' gotten Callahan pretty near to the bonanza afore he turned on him. There was a trick in it some place. We can easily follow the trail back to where Dusty first fastened Callahan to that horse: the marks of Callahan's trailin' body'll be clear enough. Just a slim chance the bonanza might be somewheres near the spot where Dusty got th' upper hand. Let's go see.'

He looked down once more at Dusty's dead body then leapt to the saddle of the horse, his colleague behind him. He rode the animal quickly back to the spot where Dusty had begun his death ride, then at a slower pace began to follow the gouged earth and flattened grass where Callahan had also been dragged.

And so, stopping every now and again to make sure of the story in the dust at intervals — aided by the brilliant moonlight — they began to work their way back to the abandoned trail where Dusty had sprung his trick and trapped the unwary Callahan.

It was inevitable that both men came finally to the gaping hole into which Callahan had plunged. Dismounting from the horse they stood looking at the cavity — then at each other.

'Some sort of an animal trap,' Al's companion said at last shrugging. 'I guess it doesn't interest us — '

'Don't be too sure it doesn't,' Al interrupted, peering at the smashed covering intently. 'A guy who wants t'trap animals doesn't have ter use all this stuff. It'd be too strong to let an animal through anyways. There's more to it than that. I'm takin' a look.'

He slid down into the cavity and let himself drop. For a moment or two his colleague stood reflecting, then with a shrug he followed suit — to find Al busy with his matchbox.

'Gosh durn it if it isn't it!' Al whispered, fascinated as he gazed around him. 'The luck's on our side, Dave! Take a look! Tons of the blasted stuff! That old twister musta covered the hole up and Callahan was the one who broke it through — Yuh know what this means? We're millionaires! An' nobody to share it with now Carson's gone.'

'Uh-huh . . . ' Dave was looking about him at the yellow metal. 'I guess yore right. It's whittled down to just us two. Maninza's the only one we need to bother about.'

'To hell with her. We can soon deal with her.' Al mused for a moment. 'Kinda queer we've seen nothin' of her — Wonder if anything's happened to her? Not as it matters, I reckon.'

He struck another match and then turned to meet Dave's greedy eyes.

'Come t'think of it,' Al said slowly, 'it's a case of finder's keepers, ain't it? I found this place, even it were an accident. All yore doin' is just cashin' in on my good luck. You said back there that yuh was sick of lookin' fur the gold. Remember?'

'Yeah, I remember.' Dave licked his lips as he saw Al draw his gun slowly in the light of the match. 'But I was only kiddin', Al. Yuh can't blame me fur — '

'I'm not blamin' yuh for anything,' Al murmured, a snaky glint in his eyes. 'I'm just thinkin' that I'd be a dad-blamed fool to share everythin' I've got with you. Yuh'd stick a knife in me ribs at the first opportunity! An' if I let yuh get away frum here you'll take with yuh the infurmation where this mine is. You get me?'

'Wait a minnit!' Dave panted, sweating. 'I guess yuh can't do this ter me! I'm yuh closest pardner, Al! Yuh can't! yuh *can't*, I tell yuh!'

* * *

Back on the rimrock Sheriff Hawkins, Val, Rod, Bill, and the gathered men stood looking down on the valley. Behind them was the smoke-filled cave from which they had emerged after exploding away the fissure to release Rod and Bill.

'I'll swear I saw a light down there,' Hawkins said, for the second time. 'Ways off in the distance there, near the edge of the foothill trees. Sort of light you might see if somebody lit a cigarette. Even a glimmer can be seen for miles in this air, remember.'

'What about it?' Bill Tandrill asked bluntly. 'Our main concern is to get Miss Kent back to town where she can catch up on some sleep — then the rest of us can start lookin' for Dusty.'

'Yeah, but that light that flashed down there might have something to *do* with Dusty,' the sheriff pointed out. 'I can't think why anybody but a renegade should need to be striking a match ways out there. Might even be Callahan — the guy who Miss Kent tells us snatched the old timer.'

'That's possible,' Rod agreed. 'Since

we've got to go down from here anyways it can't do us any harm to take a look. Come on.'

The horses were mounted and the journey along the narrow dangerous trail began. Once the safest point of the sloping mountain side had been reached the party allowed themselves more freedom and sped the horses forward, breaking into a gallop when at last they reached the almost flat, rocky ground which intervened between the mountain range proper and the forest half a mile distant.

All the time they moved, Sheriff Hawkins kept his eye on the approximate point where he had seen the glimmer of flame — but before it was reached something else took his attention. A dark and sprawling shape under the waning moon. He leapt down from the saddle quickly and hurried over to where the body lay.

'I guess it's the old feller,' he said grimly, looking up as Rod came over to him. 'From the look of things his skull's stoved in. Somebody musta given him the hell of a beatin' to do that.'

Rod clenched his fists as he looked about him. The rest of the party came riding up and sat looking in silence at the body of the dead prospector.

'That's the end of finding where that bonanza is, anyways,' Val said at length. 'Nobody else is going to find out anything and neither are we. I'd certainly like to know what Callahan did to Dusty to smash him up like this too.'

'I can tell you what he did,' Rod said bitterly, at the end of his survey in the moonlight. 'Take a look at this ground around here. It's ploughed up in the dust. There's only one answer to it — That dirty coyote Callahan musta given the old timer a death ride to make him talk. Whether he did or not I don't know, but he sure died anyway.'

'What d'yuh suppose Callahan struck a match for?' one of the deputies asked.

'Mebbe to check up on Dusty's injuries; mebbe to light a cigarette — Mebbe anything. What I want to find out is where the skunk is now so's I can settle accounts with him. There's a trail clearly marked here, sheriff. We might follow it and see where it gets us.'

'OK.' Hawkins turned to one of his men. 'You take Dusty's body back to town, Hank,' he instructed. 'He'll get a decent burial later.'

With that he swung round his horse's head and followed in the wake of Rod, the girl, and the others as they followed the trail of hoofmarks in the dying light of the moon.

'Say,' one of the deputies said at length, pointing ahead. 'I may be loco but that looks t'me like another body lying there — on th' edge of the wood.'

The men around him nodded but said nothing. In another few minutes they had dismounted and were looking at the corpse of Callahan in his tattered shirt and pants.

'I'll be dad-blamed,' the sheriff muttered. 'What d'you make of this, Gayland? Looks like Callahan got it even worse than th' old timer, and we've been blamin' him for it!'

'I don't get it,' Rod muttered. 'Damned if I do. Looks like there's more guys in on this than we — '

The distant explosion of a gun halted him in mid-sentence. He swung to look into the moonlit grey from where the report had come. As he did so it came again. Then there was silence.

'Somewheres over there,' Val said urgently, pointing. 'In what looks to be pastureland or something . . . '

Without removing her eyes from the spot where she imagined the shot had come she spurred her horse forward, and instantly the remainder of the party leapt to their saddles and followed her. They began to slow down as at first they beheld only emptiness — then Rod pointed to a cavernous hole gaping in the ground some twenty-five yards distant.

'Only likely spot,' he said. 'Take it easy while I have a look — ' He paused, watching as a massive dark shape rose suddenly out of the long grass. Half pulling his gun he hesitated, then

Hawkins gave an ejaculation.

'Somebody's cayuse has bin having a sleep! I guess we're on to somethin', Rod.'

'That's the mount Callahan was using,' Val said quickly, peering at it. 'A piebald. I remember it.'

Rod motioned for silence and then slipped down from the saddle. His gun — a borrowed one — firmly in his hand he began to advance stealthily towards the hole in the trail, going down on to his hands and knees as he reached it, then advancing until he could just peer over the edge.

He frowned at what he saw. A solitary cowpuncher was striking matches and looking about him, the dim glimmer casting now and again on the sprawled body of a second puncher lying on the floor.

'Al!' Rod half whispered to himself. 'I'll be durned! How in heck did he ever get out — ?'

He jerked his head back as, unexpectedly, a pebble dislodged itself and rolled into the hole. Instantly Al whirled, the match extinguishing simultaneously. He fired at the momentary blob of Rod's head outlined against the moonlight and for Rod the world exploded in white fire which foundered in darkness.

Immediately Sheriff Hawkins jolted his horse forward, but before he could reach the gap Al had vaulted upwards and, half concealed in the vegetation and rubbish, fired his gun again. Hawkins' horse went down with a shattered foreleg, dropping the sheriff into the dust.

'I'll shoot th' first one uv yuh that makes a wrong move!' Al grated at them, slowly rising. 'Git down frum them saddles, th' lot uv yuh — an' drop your hardware as yuh come towards me.'

'You can't get away with this, whoever you are,' Hawkins snapped. 'There are too many of us for you to handle.'

'Think so, Tinbadge? Yuh'd be surprised what I can handle when I'm in the mood! I'm aimin' straight at the gal there, and she goes out like a light if any uv yuh start tryin' anythin'! Now start walkin' as I told yuh! You first, Tinbadge.'

Al moved a little to one side, both his guns ready, watching Hawkins as he advanced in the moonlight, dropping his cross-over belts and holsters as he came.

'Down in that hole and make it quick!' the gunman ordered.

Hawkins obeyed — and one by one each of the party was compelled to perform the same actions. Just what Al was driving at remained a mystery. It was an equal mystery as to who he was. He kept his hat so well pulled down over his face it was impossible to identify him in the dim light — and his voice gave nothing away. It was as coarse as that of thousands of cow-punchers.

'You too,' he ordered to Val, as she came last. 'Down yuh git — '

As she hesitated, looking at Rod's

sprawled figure, Al aimed a blow at her. In ducking it she lost her balance and dropped below, Sheriff Hawkins' strong arms breaking her fall.

'Naterally,' Al said sourly, looming over the edge of the hole, 'yore all a-wonderin' what I'm gettin' at — ? I'll tell yuh. Right now yore in a bonanza, see? The one old Dusty Morgan had an' which I've found fur myself. Yuh'll find th' body of Dave Meadows amongst yuh: he figgered he could muscle in on some uv the gold too, but I changed his mind fur him . . . Same as I changed Callahan's mind — an' also took care uv Dusty. Nobody else has gotta know about this bonanza, see, 'cos that'd make it tough on me — So I'm surrounding yuh with gold an' killin' yuh at the same time. Good idea, huh? I'm goin' ter set fire to this vegetation and push it in the hole. Yuh'll roast, the whole stinkin' lot uv yuh, an' if yuh don't do that yuh'll smother. Later I'll come back and collect. The fire won't harm the gold even though it takes care uv you.'

There was an aghast silence from below as they realized who he was. Al chuckled and took his matchbox from his pocket. At the same moment he paused as something snaked round his ankle. He kicked impatiently, thinking it was a ground rat — then the soft movement changed to an iron grip and he was abruptly flung on to his face, the matchbox flying out of his hand.

The moment he landed he twirled round and fired savagely, and missed. A boot came up and hit him in the jaw with a force sufficient to break it. Half senseless with the blow he stared mistily at the looming figure of Rod swaying against the dawn light.

'Get up,' Rod whispered. 'Get up! You low-down, filthy son of a buzzard! I reckon you stink more'n Carson, or Callahan, or any of the others ever did — *Get up, blast you!*' he yelled.

Al got up slowly, then jerked up his gun. He could not fire it. Rod's own weapon flashed fire at the same instant and Al felt his palm go numb and swell suddenly with blood as a slug tore clean through it.

'You figgered you'd killed me, didn't you?' Rod breathed, moving over to him slowly. 'Mebbe you might have done if I'd been a fraction further over the hole. All you did was crease my scalp and I guess that'll heal up fast enough — Right now I'm going to settle with you, an' I don't mean with guns!'

He holstered his gun as he spoke and then lashed up a haymaker. Al absorbed it right on the nose and went staggering backwards. He saved himself from overbalancing and, useless though his one hand was, came charging in to the attack. Rod waited and aimed a terrific left — but at the last second Al twisted and Rod completely missed his mark. Instead he took a blow in the face that rocked him and dropped him to his knees.

'Smart, ain't yuh?' Al demanded venomously, and dived for his fallen gun. 'I'll durned soon show yuh — '

He whipped the weapon into his left hand and levelled it — then he gave a gasp of pain as a long, tough branch of the vegetation near the hole seemed to shoot out of space and hit him across the eyes. Stunned, he crashed on to his back and lay still.

'Guess that'll teach him,' Sheriff Hawkins panted, raising himself out of the hole until he stood up, then tossing aside the branch he had wielded as a weapon. 'He can be taken care of from now on . . .'

He went over to Rod and helped him up. One by one the party struggled upwards and came over to where Rod was rubbing his face bemusedly.

'You all right, Rod?' Val asked anxiously, gripping his arm — and he grinned in the dawn light.

'Yeah — just about. But I guess you and I both need a little fixing up and a durned good rest.'

'You got something there,' Bill Tandrill agreed. 'An' say, sheriff, what happens about this gold we literally dropped into? Who gets it?'

'The authorities, I guess.' The sheriff hauled Al to his feet and slung him like a sack over the saddle of his horse, roping his wrists and ankles under the animal's belly.

'We gone through all this to make the Government rich?' Rod asked hopelessly.

'There's a salvage reward — ' Hawkins mused. 'Mebbe around twenty-five per cent. That'll tot up to a good bit on a bonanza this size.'

'Yeah . . . ' Rod reflected, his arm about Val's shoulders. 'I reckon we'll find a use for it, Val,' he murmured. 'Help build up the ranch we'll *both* be running from now on, huh?'

She did not answer but Rod felt her press closer against him.

We do hope that you have enjoyed reading this large print book.

Did you know that all of our titles are available for purchase?

We publish a wide range of high quality large print books including:
Romances, Mysteries, Classics
General Fiction
Non Fiction and Westerns

Special interest titles available in large print are:
The Little Oxford Dictionary
Music Book, Song Book
Hymn Book, Service Book

Also available from us courtesy of Oxford University Press:
Young Readers' Dictionary
(large print edition)
Young Readers' Thesaurus
(large print edition)

For further information or a free brochure, please contact us at:
Ulverscroft Large Print Books Ltd.,
The Green, Bradgate Road, Anstey,
Leicester, LE7 7FU, England.
Tel: (00 44) **0116 236 4325**
Fax: (00 44) **0116 234 0205**

LAST STAGE FROM HELL'S MOUTH

Derek Rutherford

Sam Cotton is the last person anyone in the New Mexico town of Hope would have suspected of wrong-doing. All that changes, however, when he is seen riding away hell for leather from a scene of robbery and death. Though the victims' families save him from a lynching, once the judge arrives in town, Sam will stand trial for his life — with only his father believing in his innocence . . .

SKELETON PASS

John Russell Fearn

Prospecting for gold in the mountains, Pan Warlow discovers a bonanza — but does not live to enjoy his good fortune. Accidentally blowing himself up, he brings about a cataclysmic avalanche. Now he lies buried beneath a pile of rocks in Skeleton Pass — alongside $200,000 worth of gold belonging to wealthy banker Lanning Mackenzie. Lanning's daughter Flora is determined to find the treasure, aided by her Aunt Belinda, Dick Crespin and Black Moon. But she is in danger from the notorious outlaw Loupe Vanquera . . .

DEAD MAN'S CANYON

Terrell L. Bowers

After the Civil War, former ranger Nicolas Kilpatrick and his fellow ex-soldiers continue to deploy their skills, protecting settlers from Indian attacks and tracking down gangs of robbers and rustlers. In the wake of a shootout with the murderous Maitland Guerrillas, a dying bandit offers Nick information on the gang's leader — in exchange for a promise that his soon-to-be-widow will be taken care of. Setting off to chase down Frank Maitland and keep his vow, Nick heads out to Laramie . . .